I0715937

Also by Roger Neumaier

Imprints from an Odyssey

The Cuban Girl

Alex in Deutschland

A Home in the Bitterroot

Joseph Imagines God

Poetry and Reflection

What Happened to Him

*More information about each of these books is available at
https://neumaierbooks.com*

The Green House

By Roger Neumaier

Copyright 2024 by Roger Neumaier
Published in Paperback and eBook, November 2024.

Printed in the United States of America
Library of Congress Control Number: 2024924994

ISBNs: 978-1-956920-16-1 (paperback);
978-1-956920-17-8 (eBook)

The Green House is dedicated to Solomon, Otis, Big Robert, Little Robert and all of the other wonderful staff with whom I had the opportunity to work as a part of Grace Hospital's graveyard shift during the winter of 1972 - 1973. It was during this time that I became familiar with the magic of Detroit.

Roger Neumaier

Introducing The Green House

Edith Beaulieu was born in Paris, France in the year 1889. Her father, a disciple of the innovative artist, Odilon Redon, was wonderfully creative—but not very successful. Edith's father taught her to draw and paint. However, the dark-haired, dark-eyed beauty chose not to follow her father into a career as a painter nor to become an artist's model like her mother. Instead, she was intent on avoiding the poverty that had been relentless in her parents' lives. So, in the year 1911, Edith Beaulieu sought her fortune by emigrating to the United States.

*****

Edwin Byerly was born in Detroit, Michigan in 1880. Both of his parents died from influenza when he was eighteen. Byerly invested the modest inheritance he received from his parent's estate in a series of Detroit's new automobile manufacturers. They included Continental Motors, Packard, Oldsmobile Motor Works, and the Cadillac Car Company. In 1903, he added stock in Henry Ford's new venture, The Ford Motor Company, to his investment portfolio.

In 1911, Edwin decided to buy a home in one of Detroit's affluent suburbs. He felt such an acquisition would be a statement to his friends and colleagues that he had attained financial success. Byerly ended up purchasing an elegant white brick residence on the shores of Lake St. Claire in Grosse Point, Michigan.

A month later, Byerly traveled to New York City to acquire top-of-the-line furniture that would nicely complement his new Georgian-style house. Upon checking into a room at New York City's Plaza Hotel, Byerly spotted a dark-haired, dark-eyed French chambermaid who stole his heart. Days after meeting her, Edwin Byerly proposed to, then married, Edith Beaulieu.

One week and a train ride later, Byerly carried his blushing bride over the threshold strip into his brand-new Grosse Point home. Edith Beaulieu Byerly came to love that stately home. She affectionately called it the *White House*. The couple were unable to bear children. But Edith found fulfillment in the White House's sunroom drawing and painting colorful, imaginative compositions.

*****

In 1918, Edwin Byerly purchased four newly constructed boarding houses. These room-for-rent investments were designed to cater to recently hired automobile factory workers who were coming to Detroit from America's deep south. Byerly referred to each of these four boarding house investments by the color of the building's exterior. Thus, the names of these buildings were the *Red House*, the *Blue House*, the *Yellow House*, and the *Green House*. Each boarding house had a total of eighteen rooms on its three floors. One of each building's first floor rooms was reserved to house an on-site manager.

*****

Edith and Edwin lived happily. But they did not live happily ever after. On Black Tuesday, October 29, 1929, Byerly's fortune was decimated by the stock market's collapse. Late that afternoon, a distraught Mr. Byerly jumped out of his sixth-floor office window to his death.

Edith was forced to declare bankruptcy by her creditors. As such, she had to give up her cherished White House. The only large asset she retained was the Green

House. She moved into that boarding house and became its onsite manager. Edith enlarged the manager's space by combining it with the rental room next door, treating the front room as a living quarter and the newly attached back room as her artist's studio. Edith spent her days in that studio producing colorful pastel drawings and lyrical oil paintings as a means of escaping the reality that her husband was dead and her cherished home had been taken from her.

Upon her husband's death, Edith stopped using his surname. She became, once again, Edith Beaulieu. As she aged, she rarely communicated with others in or out of the Green House. One of the few people Edith continued to stay in touch with after her husband passed was her art dealer. During the 1920s, his gallery displayed and sold her artwork. After Edith moved into the Green House, he continued to represent her, selling her works to art enthusiasts across metropolitan Detroit. Her paintings gained an enthusiastic local following. A 1939 review of her work in the *Detroit Free Press* described her paintings as "visionary works tying together the worlds of dreams, flowers, and phantoms."

Edith Beaulieu never got over losing the White House. When speaking of its loss, she described the elegant Grosse Point mansion as having been stolen from her by the capitalists and the courts. The man who purchased the home (and all of its furnishings) from a bankruptcy court was a mid-level executive at General Motors. As a part of his acquisition, he became the owner of many of Edith Beaulieu's finest and most imaginative oil paintings and pastels.

Edith's second cousin, Jeannine, lived in Paris. On vacation trips to the United States in 1947 and 1949, Jeannine visited Edith and the two relatives hit it off. When Edith passed away in 1951, her will identified Jeannine as her estate's sole beneficiary. Upon learning that she had inherited the rooming house, Jeannine emigrated from Paris to Detroit, moved into the Green House, and became its manager.

****

In the years that followed Edith Beaulieu's passing, one Green House resident believed that the Green House was haunted by Edith's ghost. That boarder, a young immigrant from Eastern Europe named Ossia, was an artist. Ossia spent most of her waking hours painting and drawing in her Green House room. Ossia claimed she had a cordial relationship with Edith's spirit and believed that Edith visited her in her room and gave her constructive criticism on how to improve her artistic compositions.

Thus, the Green House was the home not only of a building manager and up to sixteen tenants, but one of those tenants believed the boarding house was also inhabited by a ghost.

Discovering the Green House

It was March of 1961 and Rusty Nolan was out looking for a room to rent. A sharp, cold wind was blowing and dark clouds threatened snow. Rusty was about to call it an afternoon and head back to his room at the Detroit YMCA when he noticed a modest structure sitting in between two much larger brick apartment buildings. The green three-story building looked like it might be a rooming house. Rusty decided to check it out before ending the day's search.

Rusty walked up to the building's front door and looked through its glass window down a hallway lined with numbered doors. Printed above the number *11* on the first door on the left was the word *Manager*. Rusty pushed the doorbell button. A moment later, a woman came out of room number *11*. She had short curly black hair, blue cat eye-framed glasses, and wore a black sweater and slacks.

"How may I assist you?" the woman asked.

Rusty noted the woman had a strong accent—maybe she was French?

He responded, "I'm looking for a room. Do you have any vacancies?"

"Please enter," she said. "It's cold out here."

Rusty stepped into the hallway of the building.

The woman asked, "Are you employed?"

"Uhm yeah—yes, I am, mam. I just started a couple of days ago at Grace Hospital. I'm an orderly. I work the graveyard shift."

"And where were you employed before Grace Hospital?"

Rusty sighed and thought to himself, *I might as well tell her the truth and get it over with. It'll probably end any chance that she'll rent me a room. But what else can I do?*

"I spent the last 18 months at Marquette—in the State prison," he told her. "And no. I wasn't an employee there."

As Rusty began to turn his body away, preparing to leave the rooming house, the woman said, "You would not be my first lodger who has been in prison before residing here. Why were you," she paused, "a guest at the jail?"

Rusty took a deep breath as he thought to himself, *Keep it simple here.*

"I got in a fight," he said. "The cops found a marijuana cigarette in my pocket. Double trouble—you know."

The woman looked up at Rusty. (He was just short of six feet tall and she was almost a foot shorter).

"No, I don't know, young man," she responded. "Not at all. I do, however, understand that you were not so smart to get into trouble like that. Still, you have been punished already."

The woman gave Rusty a short studious look before saying, "OK. No drinking, no drugs, no women in your chamber. Always respect the house's quiet time. It begins at nine in the evening." She took a deep breath and added, "And no trouble—at all. If these rules work for you, I'll show you the room."

Rusty gave a soft smile and responded, "Thank you, mam. That's more than fair."

"Please wait here," she said.

The woman went back into room 11, returning a moment later holding a key ring that had two keys and a white wooden tag. Printed on it was the number *34*. The woman led Rusty down the hall to the back of the building and up an unpainted wooden stairway. Next to the stairwell on each floor, Rusty noticed a Frigidaire refrigerator.

The woman saw Rusty look at the second-floor refrigerator and said, "Each floor has an icebox. Use the Frigidaire as you like. Never take another person's provisions."

When they got to the third floor, the woman knocked on the door across from the stairwell. There was no answer and she opened the door. Rusty saw a small bathroom. It had a porcelain toilet with a black wooden seat, a pedestal wash basin (with a dripping faucet), and a metal shower. The only color in the room came from a pink shower curtain.

"First-floor tenants are all women," she said. "Second and third-floor residents are men. Those on each floor use only their own floor's WC."

Then the woman led Rusty down the hall to a room with the number *34*. Using a key from the key ring she had retrieved from her apartment, she unlocked and opened the door. The room was lit by one window and a single ceiling light bulb. Its furnishings were a double bed, a small table, two ladderback chairs, and a chest of drawers. There was a hotplate on top of the table and a pot, a pan, and a small beaten-up aluminum coffee pot on a shelf below it.

"The monthly charge is twenty dollars—in advance," she said. "Today is the sixth. You pay just fifteen dollars for the rest of this month. Required also, however, is a deposit of twenty dollars. I will return that amount if the chamber is clean and you have given two weeks' notice before you depart. Rent is due five days before the beginning of the month."

Rusty pulled a worn brown leather wallet from the back pocket of his faded blue jeans. He opened it and removed three ten-dollar bills and a five-dollar bill.

He handed the cash to her as he said, "Thank you, mam. I'll gladly take the room. Do the blankets, pillow, and sheets that are on the bed stay?"

She examined the bills, put them in her pants pocket, and handed Rusty the keys before saying, "The bedding and two towels remain in the chamber. In the future, call me Jeannine, if you please. And your name?"

"My name's Rusty, Jeannine. Rusty Nolan."

She paused and smiled before saying, "*Bien venue a' chez moi, Monsieur* Rusty. You move into the Green House *ce soir?*"

He chuckled and said, "*Absolutement, Madame. Absolutement. Je vais récupérer mes affaires maintenant.*"

Jeannine gave a pleasant smile. "*Vous parlez Francais?*"

"*Oui, Madame. Un peu.*"

She smiled at Rusty, then turned and headed back down the hall to the stairway.

So Lonesome I Could Die

Rusty paid his last day's room charge at the YMCA and headed out the door, his stuffed duffle bag slung over his shoulder. A light snow was falling as he headed back to the Green House. As he walked, Rusty hummed Johnny Horton's "North to Alaska." Halfway to his new home, Rusty stopped at a small local grocery store and bought a can of chili, a box of soda crackers, a quart of milk, a box of sugar-frosted flakes, and a can of Folgers Coffee. Next to the market, Rusty stopped at a small liquor store and purchased a pint of Jim Beam. He figured Jeannine wouldn't catch one of her boarders if he took an occasional quiet sip of whiskey.

*****

After a satisfying dinner of canned chili and saltine crackers, Rusty lay down on his bed contemplating the day's success. What a coup! His new home was only ten blocks from work and his monthly rent was far more affordable than he'd anticipated.

He glanced at his General Electric alarm clock. It was barely 8:30. He had a couple of hours before it would be time to leave for work. Rusty reached for the pint of Jim Beam and was about to take a sip when he heard something special. Someone was playing Hank Williams' soulful recording of "I'm So Lonesome I Could Die." It sounded like it might be coming from the next room.

Rusty smiled, thinking, *The guy in the next room has awfully good taste. Time to introduce myself.*

Before knocking on room 32's door, Rusty stood and listened for a moment to more of the mournful voice and the song's heartfelt lyrics.

The silence of a falling star
Lights up a purple sky
And as I wonder where you are
I'm so lonesome, I could cry.

What a song, he thought. *What a voice.*

Rusty hoped his neighbor would be welcoming, maybe even invite him to spend some time listening to other Hank Williams recordings. He knocked on the door. The singing and the soulful sound of the slide guitar stopped.

"Come on in," said a voice with a heavy cowboy country twang.

Rusty opened the door. A skinny, unshaven middle-aged man was sitting on the side of his bed in an undershirt and boxer shorts holding a steel Dobro guitar. The man's body was bent and his head leaned forward over the Dobro.

He looked up and slowly said, "Can-I-help-you-buddy?"

"I'm your new next-door neighbor," said Rusty. "I heard the Hank Williams recording. I dig his music. But I didn't mean to have you shut off your—"

Rusty stopped speaking. He surveyed the room. There was no phonograph; no radio. His neighbor sat holding the slide guitar, waiting for Rusty to finish his thought. It had been this guy singing, he realized, backing himself up on his Dobro.

Rusty completed his statement. "I didn't mean to—uhm—have you stop—uh—singing. I've always appreciated that song." Rusty chuckled and added, "I actually thought you were playing the Hank Williams recording. But you were singing, weren't you?"

The guy chuckled, reached over to a bedside table, and picked up a lit cigarette. He took a deep drag, blew it out, and replied, "You got it, buddy. Grab a chair. What's your name? People call me *Tex*."

Rusty sat down on one of one of Tex's ladderback chairs. "The name's Rusty," he said. You know, like an old, worn-out shovel."

Tex chuckled again and said, "I've broken a few of them."

Rusty continued, "I'm sorry I interrupted you, Tex. I love that song. If you're willing, I'd appreciate it if you'd finish it."

For the next half an hour, Tex sang an assortment of Hank Williams' country hits including "Your Cheating Heart," "Honky Tonk Blues," and "Hey Good Looking." As he sang, Tex slid the glass pipe on his left hand's middle finger up and down along the neck of the Dobro. Together, his voice and slide guitar produced a haunting rendition of those wonderful Hank Williams classics.

When Tex stopped playing, he leaned his guitar against the wall next to his bed and said, "It's getting pretty late. I have to turn in. I work the early shift at Clark Street Assembly—you know, making those Cadillacs beautiful. Pleasure to meet you, Rusty. Welcome to the Green House."

"I was lucky there was a vacancy," said Rusty.

"Oh, there's always a couple of vacancies around this place," said Tex with a chuckle. "It's just that Jeannine, well, she's cautious about who she'll accept as a boarder."

Rusty thought that was odd since Jeannine hadn't been bothered by the fact he was an ex-con. He was just glad he'd met whatever requirements Jeannine had in place for new residents.

Rusty stood up and said, "It's been good to meet you, Tex. Thanks for the personal concert and the warm welcome. I hope I'll get to hear more of your music in the future."

Tex replied, "On Saturday evenings, I sing a few songs at Tony's Tavern near Wayne State. Green House compadres sometimes tag along with me. I'll leave here around seven this Saturday. If you're interested, why don't you join me?"

"That's great," said Rusty. "Count me in."

As Rusty returned to his room, he thought, *This is my lucky day. I got a place next door to a country western performer!*

Grace Hospital

After returning to his room, Rusty glanced at his alarm clock. It was almost ten. He had half an hour before he needed to leave for work. That was enough time for a cup of coffee.

He picked up the small aluminum stove-top percolator and examined it. It was pretty beaten up. But its coffee basket was still intact. He rinsed the pot, filled it with a couple of cups of water, opened the can of Folgers, and placed three heaping spoons of sweet-smelling coffee grounds into the pot's brewing basket. Then he put the percolator on the hotplate which he turned to high. Several minutes later, Rusty was savoring a fresh cup of java in his new home.

That evening, Rusty's ten-minute walk to Grace Hospital was especially peaceful. While it was cold outside, there was no wind and the snow had stopped falling. As he walked, Rusty thought about how lowering his room rent, fixing his meals in his room, and walking (rather than taking the bus) would significantly take the pressure off of his finances.

*****

A few weeks before, Rusty had been thrilled when he was offered a job at Grace Hospital. Grace was the area's leading hospital for patients suffering from chronic conditions. It also was the site of Detroit's primary emergency room. Grace Hospital orderlies supported both regular hospital and emergency room services.

Rusty entered Grace Hospital's old brick building and went directly to the employee locker room. He changed into light blue hospital scrubs and proceeded to the nearby orderlies' room. Rusty's supervisor, Otis, and a couple of orderlies were already there making small talk and listening to Otis' radio which was tuned to the sounds of gospel, rhythm, and blues on WKNR.

As Rusty sat down, Otis asked him, "How's it going, man? Find a place yet?"

"I did," Rusty responded with a big grin. "I scored; found a room about ten blocks up on the other side of Woodward. Only twenty bucks a month! The place is clean and the room's got a hot plate and a sink!"

"Where's it located?" asked Big Robert, one of the orderlies.

Rusty gave the address and said, "They call it the *Green House*,"

"Hmm," murmured Big Robert. "Green rooming house—huh? I checked that joint out six months ago. French lady who runs the place said there weren't no vacancies. You're one lucky dude, Rusty."

The phone rang and Otis answered it. After putting down the receiver, Otis turned to Rusty and said, "You're on, man. That tall good-looking white nurse up in ICU needs assistance with an overweight patient—stat."

The night's work had begun. Rusty got up from his chair and rushed up to the intensive care unit.

Assisting a change of bed sheets for a large patient (often weighing more than four hundred pounds) was a recurring assignment. The task was critical because of the danger that a weak, overweight invalid might roll off the bed. That was why an orderly was always present holding a large patient steady during a sheet change.

To successfully change a bedsheet, the patient had to be rolled onto their side. The old sheet was pulled out from their backside and tucked tightly behind the patient while a fresh sheet was placed onto that empty half of the bed. Then the patient was rolled over onto their other side, the old sheet was pulled off the bed, and the clean sheet was unfurled and tucked into the mattress. Presto, the sheet change was complete.

After helping the nurse change the bedding, Rusty walked back to the orderlies' room. As he walked, he thought about his conversation with Jeannine. He felt guilty for lying to her about the reason he'd been serving time. But if he'd been honest; if he'd told her the real reason he'd done time? Well, she probably wouldn't have rented him the room.

Rusty didn't like telling a lie. Still, a man's gotta do what a man's gotta do.

Tony's Bar

Rusty had the weekend off but would stay in his room the whole time because he had only three one-dollar bills left in his wallet. He'd be fine. Monday was payday and he could ration out his last can of beef stew until then. He'd entertain himself Saturday and Sunday evenings listening to the Pistons play basketball on the Motorola radio he'd purchased at Goodwill earlier in the week.

Late Saturday afternoon, he was resting on his bed when there was a knock on the door.

"Come on in."

The door opened. It was Tex.

"Like I said, I perform this evening at Tony's Bar. John, from the second floor, is gonna meet me there. Wanna join us?"

"Thanks, but no thanks," said Rusty. "I'm sorta running low on funds. The deposit for this room pretty much cleaned me out."

"No problem. Tony's too cheap to pay me anything. My deal with him is a pizza and beer in exchange for country tunes. How can you pass that up? We'll have an extra-large pizza with tons of pepperoni, sausage, and mushrooms and all the Blatz or Budweiser we can drink. The bonus is that you get free entertainment! I perform two forty-five-minute sets."

Rusty gave a big smile and said, "How can I turn that down? When do we leave?"

*****

At six-thirty, Tex rapped on Rusty's door and the two men headed out to Tony's. Tex looked the part of a country western singer in a red double-breasted cowboy shirt with mother-of-pearl snaps, washed-out blue jeans and a worn sheepskin-lined denim jacket.

Since moving into the Green House, Rusty hadn't met any of its residents other than Tex and Jeannine. John who he would meet at the bar would be his third Green House acquaintance.

As Tex and Rusty walked the half mile to Tony's, Tex told Rusty about John.

"John's a little weird. He likes to pry into the lives of others and he refuses to let you know anything about him. When I don't want to answer a question he's asked about my life, I just ignore him. He gets the point. Once you move past that crap, you find out he's an OK guy—with a weird sense of humor."

Rusty chewed on that for a moment, then responded, "When I was in the joint, I met all kinds. Some of the cons played a lot of mind games. I learned to ignore their bullshit and paid attention when it was warranted. I'll plan on doing that with John. Thanks for the heads up."

*****

Tony's Bar and Pizzeria was a cross between a typical Italian-American pizza restaurant and an old-fashioned neighborhood tavern. As Tex and Rusty entered, the bartender hollered out, "Hey Tex, good to see you. You want the regular?"

Tex grinned and said, "The regular'd be great, Charlie. There are three of us tonight. And it's good to see you, too."

Rusty and Tex took a table near the stage. A few minutes later, Charlie placed three frosty mugs and a frothy pitcher of beer on their table. Tex filled two of the mugs.

"John'll be here soon," he said to Rusty. "He's always a little late—or a little early—depending upon whatever angle he happens to be working."

The cold beer hit the spot and the sounds out of the jukebox made the evening feel festive. The two housemates listened to "The Battle of New Orleans" by Johnny Horton followed by Marty Robbins' "El Paso." The jukebox music wouldn't stop playing fifties hits until later in the evening when Tex strapped on his guitar, stepped onto the stage, and began to sing.

Charlie brought over a sizzling oversized pizza smothered with sausage, pepperoni, mushrooms, olives, and onions. "Enjoy it," he said as he picked up the almost empty beer pitcher and replaced it with one so full of beer that when he placed it on the table, foam spilled out.

Before Tex or Rusty could reach for a piece of pizza, a medium-height man wearing an oversized army surplus trench coat and a black stocking cap walked up to the table, pulled out a chair, and spun it around so he could straddle it.

As he sat down with his hands resting on the back of the wooden chair, the man said, "Hey Tex, how's it playing? Who's your buddy?"

As Tex filled the third mug, slid it over to the guy in the trench coat, and topped off Rusty and his mugs, he replied to the question. "Couldn't be much better, John. This here's Rusty. He just moved into 34."

"Pleased to meet you, Rusty. Ossia told me you moved in."

"Who's Ossia?" asked Rusty.

John took a long drink of beer from his mug, wiped his mouth with the back of his right hand, and gave a soft belch before he responded to Rusty.

"Too long a story for a Friday night," he said.

John reached over, grabbed a plate, and helped himself to the largest, meatiest piece of pizza. Tex and Rusty followed his lead by each taking a piece.

Rusty hadn't had pizza since he'd gotten out of prison. It tasted awfully good.

"This is great pizza," he said. "And nice-looking trench coat, John. You spend much time in the army?"

"Nope," was John's response. "Couldn't've gotten me in there with a cattle prod. I just like a good, cheap, warm coat."

Ten minutes later, the pizza was gone and the fresh pitcher of beer emptied. Tex reached down for his guitar case. Minutes later, he was up on the bar's small stage and was greeted with a warm round of applause from the bar's patrons. Without acknowledging the clapping, Tex moved right into "The Streets of Laredo."

*****

A couple of hours later, as the three housemates walked back to their home under a cold clear sky, Rusty asked John, "How long you been living in the Green House?"

John kept walking for a couple of minutes before responding. "I've been here about five years. It's cheap, clean and people mind their own business—which I like a lot."

Rusty followed this up by asking, "Do you work in the area?"

John turned to Tex and said, "Your friend sure asks a lot of questions, doesn't he?"

Tex responded, "Sort of stealing your thunder, eh?"

They walked for a while in silence.

"I understand you recently got out of the joint," said John. "What were you doing time for?"

Rusty turned to Tex and said, "Well Tex, I guess I'm not the only person you know who likes to ask a lot of questions."

*****

Sunday morning, Rusty went to Tex's room. After thanking Tex for including him the previous evening, Rusty asked, "What's John's story? He seemed defensive last night. Did I offend him?"

Tex had been changing the strings on his guitar. He paused for a moment before looking up and responding. "Like I told you, John is a little weird. I think he does the weird thing to keep people at a distance. But you get used to him. He's not that bad a dude. Just, like I said," Tex paused before finishing his thought, "he's weird."

Tex started tuning another string on the Dobro. Rusty watched and wondered if Tex would say more about John. He was about to return to his room when Tex continued speaking, stopping occasionally to adjust, then listen to, each guitar string.

"I've known John for a couple of years. It wasn't until a few months ago he said anything about himself. He told me his dad was in the army—pretty high up. John said his pop expected John to be the perfect child. But John didn't really meet that test. His dad wasn't so happy about it. When John was still pretty young, he told me his dad went off to fight against the fuehrer. John said he never saw his father again, that his dad died in the war. That sort of impressed me until Ossia told me John and his dad aren't speaking with one another. I asked Ossia what John's dad did. Ossia said he was a rich investor. So, based upon all that, I don't have too much of a clue about John's past. But my advice? I wouldn't take anything that dude says to the bank."

Tex chuckled before adding, "Ossia told me that John likes to write. She doesn't know what he likes to write about, just that he told her he likes to do it. I heard from Jeannine that John works as a waiter in a swanky Dearborn restaurant. She said he only works there a couple days a week."

Tex put the Dobro down next to his bed and chuckled again, shaking his head from side to side, before saying. "This place can get a little strange. I often don't know who to believe. John told me Ossia has visits with this ghost—here in the Green House. Edith—that's what Ossia calls the ghost—she's supposedly the spirit of the lady who owned this place when it was new. According to Ossia, Edith lived here for a few decades before she kicked the bucket. Ossia told John that Edith shows up in her room and speaks with her—often. Pretty strange—wouldn't you say?"

After saying that, Tex picked up his guitar, placed a glass slide onto his left hand's middle finger, then softly touched the slide onto the Dobro neck's strings and began to play "Tumblin Tumbleweed."

As he played, he softly sang the words. After the last chorus of *drifting along with the tumbling tumbleweed*, he stopped playing but did not remove the guitar from his lap.

He changed the subject. "Now, John—that dude's got a pretty nice set of wheels. He's the only person in the Green House who owns a car. I don't know if John's got money or if he just spent all of his cash on that '59 Impala. Anyway, now and then, somebody from this house has got to go somewhere and John gives 'em a lift. I don't know too much more about him than that."

Then Tex went into an instrumental rendition of "Your Cheating Heart" on the slide guitar. After that, they sat in silence.

After a couple of minutes, Rusty asked, "Tell me more about Ossia."

"What I know about Ossia is what John and Jeannine have told me. She has had a pretty tough life, had some awfully frightening things happen to her during the war—done first by the Nazis, then by the Soviets. I don't know more details than that. Now, the woman just paints pictures in her room. Except for Jeannine and John, Ossia pretty much seems to keep to herself. My guess is John knew about your being in the joint because Jeannine told Ossia and then John wheedled the information out of her."

Tex leaned his guitar against the wall next to his bed before saying, "I don't know how John and Ossia became friends. Anyway, they did—or at least, John says they did. He said they have tea together—can you believe it—tea? John said he sits there and they talk about all sorts of things while Ossia paints."

Tex paused, then added, "I think John and Ossia get along well because they're both weird."

Meeting Ossia

Between rowing camaraderie at work and the peacefulness of the Green House, Rusty was pleased how his life had become more pleasant while the haunting memories of eighteen long hard months in a state prison continued to fade.

Rusty's work schedule gave him every third weekend off. He spent his free Saturday evenings at Tony's Bar eating pizza, drinking beer, and listening to Tex's country western performances. During those evenings, John seemed to have become more prone to thoughtful conversations and less likely to be sarcastic.

*****

One Sunday morning, Rusty was waiting in the Packer Foods Grocery checkout line with his standard fare of chili, beef stew, coffee, eggs, and bacon. Rusty recognized the middle-aged woman in a dark wool coat standing in line behind him. Though her face and light brown hair were mostly covered by a large red and white scarf, he was certain who she was.

Rusty turned to Ossia and said, "Hi. I recognize you from the Green House. My name's Rusty. I live in 304. OK if we walk back to the Green House together?

Ossia shyly bent her head down, almost as if she were examining her feet; then said with a heavy Eastern European accent, "Yes, I Ossia. Jeannine speak about you, Rusty. Agree. Would be nice—walk together."

A few minutes later, Ossia and Rusty, each carrying their bag of provisions, silently made their way back to the Green House. While it had been drizzling earlier, all of the rain had stopped and the sun was peeking out from behind the clouds.

As they turned off of Warren Avenue, Ossia pointed at the sky above the Green House and said, "Good sign."

Rusty looked up and saw a bright rainbow, one end of which seemed to come out of their rooming house. The red, orange, yellow, green, and blue layers of the misty arc seemed to sparkle.

"Wow," he said. "That's about as beautiful a rainbow as I've ever seen. You're right, Ossia. My mom always said *Rainbows mean good fortune.*"

They finished their walk to the Green House without more words. Rusty unlocked the front door and held it open for Ossia. They walked down the hallway and when they reached room 16, Ossia pulled a key from her small handbag and said, "You return, five minutes? We drink tea?"

Rusty gave a big smile and said, "Yes, Ossia. That would be my pleasure."

*****

When Rusty returned, he was impressed by how spacious Ossia's room felt. It may have been the same size as his but it seemed so much bigger. Instead of a double bed, she had a twin bed pushed against a wall. Next to it was a small cabinet with a sink and a hotplate. Across the room was a small red velvet upholstered settee with a matching chair and a coffee table. In the center of her room were a wooden painter's easel and a small paint-splotched wooden cart. On it were paint brushes, small jars of cloudy liquids, and a series of halfway-squeezed tubes of paint.

Rusty was struck by the partially complete canvas sitting on her easel. On the left side of the composition was a bouquet of brightly colored flowers over which blue butterflies hovered. On the right was a sketched drawing of a woman sitting in a chair, her head bent as if in grief. The chair in the painting looked like the one sitting next to the settee. Rusty stopped and stared at that painting for almost a minute, suddenly becoming aware and embarrassed that the artwork had caused him to ignore his hostess.

"I'm so sorry," he said, shaking his head as if trying to remove cobwebs from his brain. "I'm stunned by that oil painting, Ossia. It's powerful—unusual—almost haunting." He paused, smiled, and added, "Thank you for inviting me to your home."

"Thank you for praise; also, for accept invitation. Please sit," she said while pointing at the settee.

Ossia went to her small kitchen cabinet and returned with a large pink and yellow teapot and a red plate covered with ginger snap cookies. She placed these in front of Rusty on the small table and retraced her steps, returning with a pink mug and a blue one.

Ossia sat on her chair and was about to pour tea when Rusty said, "The table, the colorful teapot, and cups together with the red plate of brown cookies look like a Matisse painting."

"Thank you," she said. With a big smile, she asked, "Know art?"

"One of my escapes," he said, "during my incarceration at the state prison was paging through art books in the inmate library. That was a way I could escape—at least in my mind's eye—from the environment in which I was living. I enjoyed those bright colorful images from nineteenth-century France. The colors in your studio remind me of some of those French artists' works. I was so inspired by their art that I actually took French language classes in the prison library taught by a community volunteer."

"Jeannine say you be in prison."

Rusty chuckled. "I've discovered that word quickly gets around in the Green House."

Ossia took a deep breath and looked down. When she looked up, she gave a serious look and said, "Horrible be prisoner, Rusty. I know. I spend years in locked rooms—during war and after. Lose freedom is lose color in life."

Responding to the pain in Ossia's voice, Rusty said, "I'm sorry, Ossia."

"Yes," Ossia said. "It horrid. Not for discuss today. Someday I speak."

Rusty nodded. "And I will tell you about myself as well. I would enjoy becoming your friend."

Ossia smiled, then looked down as she poured tea into their mugs. She handed the blue mug to Rusty saying, "Take cookie, please."

Five minutes of silence followed. Rusty didn't know what sort of tea it was. However, he liked its fragrance and delicate flavor. And the ginger snaps sure hit the spot.

When his mug was empty, he said, "I enjoyed the tea. Could I have some more?"

As she poured the tea, Ossia said, "Jasmine my favorite. Delicacy it bring give peace. Like cookies too?"

"They are good."

"Have more."

Rusty stayed another five minutes. He was surprised at how comfortable he felt in Ossia's room. He had just met her. Yet, it seemed as if he had known her for years.

Rusty glanced at his watch, recognized he shouldn't overstay his welcome, and said, "Thank you, Ossia. I'll return your invitation soon. I don't have such a nice room and I certainly don't have such a colorful tea set. But I do look forward to getting to know you better."

"And me, you."

John's Visit

A couple of hours after returning from work one morning, Rusty's sleep was interrupted by a knock on his door. He sat up in bed and shook the cobwebs from his head.

"Uhm yeah? Is there uh—is someone there?"

A voice replied, "Hey man, it's me, John. Okay if I stop by?"

Rusty pulled his jeans on as he said, "Sure, John. C'mon in."

The door opened. John entered. The room was rocked with a sweet scent which Rusty recognized from his time at Marquette. John's demeanor confirmed that what Rusty had smelled was marijuana.

"What's happening?" asked John.

"Oh, I was sleeping. I work the midnight shift and just got home a little while ago."

"Sorry man. Do you want me to come back some other time?"

"No. No, I'm awake now. Was there something on your mind?"

"Yes. No. Maybe," was John's response.

Rusty's voice was tinged with irritation as he asked, "So which is it, John?"

"It's like this, Rusty. A few days ago, I was talking— talking to Ossia. And she told me—well, she said that she and you two had talked—*a nice conversation*, she called it. She mentioned you told her you'd been in the joint. I found that curious—I didn't comment on it—not to her, anyway. I just found it odd because Jeannine had also mentioned it in passing, I mean that you'd spent some time in lockup. Jeannine said you'd told her you'd gotten into a fight and happened to be carrying a joint. I was sort of curious about that because I've been in a couple of fights myself and have smoked a few joints—in fact I smoked one recently—just minutes ago. Anyway, eighteen months incarcerated? That's a pretty stiff sentence—I mean for a fight and a joint. Anyway, last week I was up in Lansing visiting a buddy. It occurred to me—heh, I'm here. I could go into the Michigan Department of Corrections headquarters and find out what exactly did transpire."

Rusty was thinking to himself, *What an asshole,* as he watched John hem and haw.

John continued, "I mean, I know it's none of my business and all. And, it's not that big a deal. I was just sort of curious. Anyway, after I filled out two or three forms and waited for half an hour or so, the lady told me, yes, you'd been in Marquette for eighteen months. However, she said you were there because you'd broken into a few homes in Ann Arbor—relieved them, so to speak, of their contents. She told me you'd gotten off early for good behavior; that you could have been under lock and key for another year and a half. Anyway, I thought that was interesting—you know—different viewpoints on what all had gone down."

There was silence in the room.

Rusty took a deep breath, exhaled, and then quietly and slowly said, "You are right John. You nailed it." He paused, then finished his statement, "It's none of your god-damned business."

Rusty stood up before angrily saying, "I *do* have one serious question for you. Who the hell do you think you are? Or, let's put this another way, what is your fucking role around this place? I mean, are you sort of the house mom? The grand inquisitor? Which is it? Each time I've seen you—that includes today, and several times at Tony's—you've been an arrogant asshole. I know it's not my *business*—to borrow your line—it's not my business to tell you this, but in the spirit of the day—embracing the open communication approach that you've taken, I might as well break it to you. You excel in your role as an arrogant asshole."

Again, silence in the room.

"Now," Rusty concluded. "I had just gone to sleep. You see, I work. I work the graveyard shift and I just got home. So, I have a brilliant idea. Why don't you hustle your inquisitive little ass out of my room? Go down, smoke some of your weed—which, last I heard was not so damn legal—and stay the hell out of my face. I am going to attempt to go back to sleep."

A shoulder-slumped John quietly left the room.

It took an agitated Rusty an hour to fall back to sleep.
*****

When Rusty awoke three hours later, he was still angry.

He lay in bed wondering, *What the hell? Is that bastard going to get me tossed out of the building? Why was Ossia saying anything to John about me? And what was Jeannine doing sharing my personal information with another one of her boarders?*

Then Rusty heard something—coming from near the door. He sat up, got out of bed, and picked up a folded piece of paper that had been slipped under the door. His name was written in pencil on the outside. After he unfolded it, he saw the following handwritten note.

Heh, Rusty,

I owe you an apology.

For starters, I have a bad habit—you weren't the first to notice—of not minding my own business. That was screwup #1. You're an interesting character. I asked both Ossia and Jeannine about you. Full disclosure, I also asked Tex. Tex told me you were an OK guy and I should "mind my own fucking business."

I should've listened to Tex.

Anyway, then came screwup #2. Yesterday, I went up to Lansing to visit an old college buddy. I was curious and went on over and inquired, like I said, at the Department of Corrections office. I might even have thrown in a lie or two as to why I was asking those questions about you.

I smoked some dope this morning. Here comes screwup #3. I got inspired. I decided to ask you about this stuff. You were right to tell me where to get off.

Anyway, I apologize for acting like such an asshole—multiple times. I'll try to control it.

John

P.S. Hope to see you Saturday at Tony's.

Rusty read the note, looked down, closed his eyes, and shook his head from side to side. Then he read the note a second time, crumbled it up, and threw it into the waste basket in the corner of his room.

"Asshole," Rusty said aloud.

Then he laid down on his bed and tried to go back to sleep.

*****

Over the next few days, Rusty worried that John would not mind his own business; that he might share what he had learned about Rusty's crime with Jeannine. Rusty had not seen anything yet that would give him confidence that John could control himself or treat others with respect.

Rusty's exact thought was, *Things have been going well at work and I'm enjoying living in the Green House. But John is someone who may be about to destroy it all.*

*****

Rusty had the weekend off. Late Saturday afternoon, he was sitting in his room trying to decide whether dinner would be a can of chili or a can of beef stew. There was a rap on his door.

Based upon his last experience with a visitor, Rusty cautiously went to the door and opened it. It was Tex.

"Hey, Rusty," Tex said, "John told me about what a jerk he was. After he told me what he'd done, I agreed with him—he's a total jerk. John said he was going to show up at

Tony's tonight. He said he hopes you'll be there as well. I sure wouldn't blame you if you decided to skip it. But I hope you join us. John may be an asshole, But once you get past that, well, you'll find out that he's an interesting asshole." Tex chuckled and added, "I'd appreciate it if you'd join us."

Rusty couldn't help but laugh. "Yeah. Thanks, Tex. Pizza and beer sounds a lot better than canned chili or beef stew. What time are you leaving? I'll walk there with you."

Tex smiled and said, "Thanks, man. I'll stop by at seven."

*****

That evening, John arrived at Tony's before Rusty and Tex.

When Rusty approached the table, John stood up, turned to him, gave a sheepish smile, and said, "I'm glad you made it."

The Portrait

On a day off in early May, Rusty was returning from a morning grocery run when he saw Ossia in the Green House's first-floor hallway.

"You visit today—drink cup of tea?" she asked.

"That'd be nice, Ossia. I'll be down after I stash my groceries."

A few minutes later, Rusty was back. When Ossia opened the door, he handed her a box of chocolate-covered cherries he had purchased in anticipation of making such a visit.

"Thank you," she said with a smile. "We enjoy today with tea. Welcome my home."

Rusty sat down on the settee as Ossia went to her hotplate. He watched as she carefully poured hot water into her pink and yellow teapot. Minutes later, she sat down and poured tea into the same pink and blue mugs they had drunk from during his first visit. She took the wrapper off of the package of chocolate-covered cherries and held the open box out to Rusty. He took one. She followed suit. Nothing was said for several minutes as they enjoyed chocolate-covered cherries and oolong tea.

After Ossia had refilled their teacups, she said, "John tell me how he play detective. I scold him. Explain I forced live with people do that in Europe. Not want it here in United States—not in any way. John apologize me. Say he make apology you. That true? Things fixed?"

Rusty chuckled. "Yes. I guess he did apologize. Still, we'll just have to find out if he is capable of keeping his nose out of anyone's business. I'm not confident."

Ossia laughed. "Truth your words. I believe he want fix but not certain he able control actions. John often not think."

Then Ossia's face took on a serious look as she said, "I need apologize also. I share things you say. Hope friendship not broken between you me?"

"I accept your apology and appreciate that you care enough to offer it. No, Ossia. The trust between us hasn't been damaged—and it won't be."

They drank their tea. Rusty noted once again how comfortable the silence was.

After a while, Ossia said, "Most times, I paint flowers, nature. But sometimes, Rusty, I make portraits. Portrait is spiritual—not just detail of face, body. Portrait image of person's soul. I only make portrait when spirit calls me. Your spirit does this. I wish paint you—make portrait of Rusty. You agree?

Rusty was quiet and looked down. As she watched him, Ossia's face took on a worried look.

When Rusty looked up, he said, "Ossia. Your offer is special. I am humbled. Yes, it would be an honor to sit for a portrait. But as you know, I work five days a week. Won't that make doing a portrait difficult?"

Ossia stood up and said, "We start now. I paint when I can. Good plan?"

Rusty smiled and said, "Excellent plan."

Ossia walked over to her paint-spackled easel which held a medium-sized square painting of a glass vase full of brightly colored lilacs, lilies, and daffodils. In the back of the composition, behind the flower arrangement, was a night sky. In a corner of the composition, was a rainbow made up entirely of shades of brown, green, and purple—no yellows, reds or oranges—nothing bright.

Ossia released the wooden piece that went across the top of her easel and removed the partially completed painting. She carried it over to a floor-to-ceiling storage cabinet located next to her small kitchenette and slid it into a vertical storage compartment. Then she removed a blank canvas of about the same size from the next compartment.

She brought the canvas to her easel and secured it with the wooden crosspiece.

Ossia walked across her room, fetched a wooden stool from the corner of her room, and placed it between the settee and the easel. "Sit on stool, Rusty," she said. "I begin."

Rusty sat down on the stool and Ossia began to sketch on the canvas with a pencil.

As she drew, Ossia spoke softly. "Making art give soul peace. Similar listening Chopin concerto. Similar watching river flow. I assemble image—record what I see, what I feel, maybe even what I dream."

Ossia paused, then said, "I live with Papa and brothers in beautiful Warsaw apartment. When I small, I discover I love art. As young girl, become famous across Warsaw for ability draw. Finish public school. Become student, Warsaw Academy for Fine Art. Great honor. Academy famous. It respected across Europe. Every morning, walk through Warsaw to Academy from home. Song in heart. Those walks, drawing classes—most happy memories."

Rusty watched her left arm quickly move across the canvas. He was amazed at the speed with which she drew and how she could speak to him as she sketched. Every now and then, Ossia would stop drawing and look at him for a moment. Then she would look back to her drawing (which Rusty could not see) and continue to work on her composition.

"You said you lived with your father and brothers. What happened to your mother?" Rusty asked.

Ossia stopped drawing, looked down, shook her head slowly from side to side, and gave a sad smile. "Mom die when I small. No memory for her. Papa? He become mom and pop for me. Two brothers? They wonderful. Me? So much love come to me as young. I lucky."

Ossia turned her attention back to the canvas.

Rusty asked, "Can I see the drawing?"

Ossia gave a coy smile and said, "No, Rusty. Sorry. Each painting, it like give birth to something unique. It private within me until complete. After portrait finish, you see it."

Rusty returned the smile and said, "I get it."

"Autumn, 1939. Begin second year drawing and painting at Warsaw Academy for Fine Art. Germany invade Poland. It horrid—unreal—frightening—nightmare. Germans march into Warsaw. Brothers quick run from home, join resistance. Papa? He stay with me. Papa not political. Still, Nazis arrest him. It make no sense, Rusty. Papa teach Polish literature; write beautiful poetry. He enemy no one. Papa kind, gentle man. I go to Warsaw Gestapo headquarter. Explain—Papa good man; not political."

She continued to draw for a while without speaking. When she stopped drawing, she turned to Rusty, sighed and said, "They arrest me."

Rusty was stunned with the terrible simplicity of what she had shared. He did not respond. He had no idea of what he could say that would be appropriate.

After fifteen minutes of silence (except for the sound of Ossia's pencil scratching across the canvas), Ossia spoke. "Thank you, Rusty, not say something with no meaning. Say nothing sometime much bigger than empty words. I not know why, but you bring peace. I enjoy draw you. I comfortable share story my life for you. In future, work on portrait, you have time. We drink tea, we talk, you sit, I paint. Today, I share you my story. Not pretty. Maybe someday, you speak your story?"

Rusty considered her request.

"Maybe, Ossia," he said. "Maybe someday."

"Thank you, Rusty. We done today," she said as she placed a piece of paint-stained fabric over the easel and canvas.

"Today, Rusty," she said, "we make good beginning—friendship and portrait. For future, we continue both. Sound good?"

"Sounds like a plan, Ossia. I don't work this Saturday. Maybe we can meet then?"

"That good. Meet Saturday morning—maybe ten?"

"That's great," Rusty said. "Have a good day." He laughed and added, "I've gotta head over to the laundromat. I've got some dirty clothes that are begging to be washed."

*****

Sunday afternoon, Rusty bought a six-pack of Schlitz Beer. That evening, he invited Tex over to his room for a beer. They started out discussing the Detroit Tigers baseball team.

Tex summed up his frustrations with his favorite team. "You'd think that with Colavito, Cash, and Kaline, the Tigers would make it to the series. But no. As long as the Yankees have Mantle and Maris, it's only a dream."

After they finished their beers, Rusty opened two more bottles of Schlitz. He handed one to Tex and said, "I ran into Ossia the other day. She's been nice to me; invited me over for a cup of tea; then told me she was gonna paint my portrait."

Tex sighed and said, "Sounds like Ossia likes you, Rusty—a whole hell of a lot more than she likes me."

The Second Sitting

Precisely at ten on the following Saturday morning, Ossia answered Rusty's knock on her door.

"Welcome, Rusty," she said. "Sketch complete. Today, begin add color portrait."

Minutes later, Rusty was seated on the stool and Ossia was intently working on the canvas.

After half an hour, as if there had not been a break from their previous conversation, Ossia said, "I never saw father, brothers again."

The magnitude of that statement took the air out of the room. A silence followed punctuated only by the sounds of brush on canvas.

A half-hour later, Ossia walked over to the hot plate and turned on the burner underneath the tea kettle. She returned to her easel and squeezed a small amount of cadmium yellow oil paint onto her palette and began to mix it with a touch of tangerine orange using a flat wooden handled palette knife. When the tea kettle started to whistle, she put down the palette knife, returned to the kettle and poured hot water into her orange and yellow teapot.

Minutes later, Ossia and Rusty were sipping mugs of mint tea with honey.

Ossia painted intensely for another half an hour. She continued to work on the canvas, occasionally looking at Rusty with a focused look before returning her attention to the canvas.

Rusty broke the quiet. "I heard you sometimes speak with a ghost."

Ossia put down her palette knife and turned toward Rusty. She smiled and said, "Sound like you not only person John like talk about."

Rusty chuckled.

Ossia picked up her tea mug and walked over to her chair by the settee. She sat down and said, "Bring mug, Rusty. Come. Sit down. Today, paint no more. We talk."

After Rusty sat down on the settee, Ossia said, "I tell about Edith ghost future day. Today, finish describe my life before Green House."

Ossia took a sip of tea and gazed across the room. Rusty could see that whatever she was remembering was painful. He waited for her to speak.

She looked up at the ceiling for a moment, then back at Rusty and said, "After Gestapo arrest, I spend weeks—maybe months—in basement, Gestapo jail. It horrid. You not able imagine cruelty Gestapo. I young, innocent. They come to cell, steal innocence, laugh. I try defend myself. I cry out. They beat me—laugh. They say awful things—laugh. I hate them. They not human. I begin wish for death."

Ossia looked straight ahead. In a quiet inexpressive manner, she said, "Gestapo send me Nazi *Arbeitslager* in South Poland. I work as slave. Sew German uniforms. Work German owned factories. Each day, work in factory. Day complete, return prison. Sleep. Next day, return factory. This continue two years, Rusty. They abuse me. I learn stop feeling. They break me, Rusty. They break me complete. I do whatever told. Spring 1943, put me on truck—like animal. Drive to Majdanek concentration camp. Abuse continue. Hope gone. Feeling gone. Do what told. Many die. I wish for death. Still, I survive. But soul of girl that study art at Warsaw Academy—it disappear—forever."

Ossia continued to tell her story to Rusty. Her voice turned into a whisper. She described how, in July of 1944, the Nazi guards ran away from Majdanek and the Soviet army arrived. Ossia was physically and emotionally too broken to celebrate. When she tried to inform her liberators about the horror she had experienced, no one heard because she spoke Polish, German, and English. The Soviets assigned to dismantle Majdanek only spoke Russian. They did not understand what she said. They showed no sympathy.

In the fall of 1945, Ossia was moved to a Prague hospital for the criminally insane. She tried again, in Polish, German, and English, to explain to the hospital staff the horror she had experienced. But she could not speak Russian, Czech, or Slovak—the languages these staff understood. Her pleas were once again ignored. Because she spoke German, her keepers determined she must be a Nazi collaborator. So, instead of compassion for the horror she had experienced, asylum staff delivered more abuse, a continuation of what she had received since being arrested by the Gestapo in Warsaw almost six years before.

After a year and a half's confinement in the Prague Hospital for the Criminally Insane, Ossia was transferred to a Frankfurt mental hospital staffed by American medical personnel. At that hospital, Ossia met an American nurse who listened to her tell of her years of horror. Ossia was given the option to relocate to the United States instead of being repatriated to her native Poland which had fallen under Soviet control. The American relocation occurred and Ossia was transported for evaluation to a Pontiac Michigan hospital for the mentally ill.

Ossia closed her eyes, took a deep breath, and slowly let it out. Then she said, "At Pontiac hospital, I tell doctor, I study art in Warsaw. He listen! Right away, place pencil, paper on table in front me. I pick up pencil, draw. Doctor understand I love art, discover create art give me peace. He realize I not crazy. I just hurt bad by evil.

American Government force Germany pay me always, every month—for destroy my life. They call payment for food, shelter, clothing *restitution*. Pontiac hospital caseworker find me place out of hospital. It the Green House. I come here. Edith Beaulieu give me love; treat me like daughter. We paint together. Edith teach me about color, images, visual magic. Edith my healer."

Rusty was stunned. Hearing about the pain Ossia had endured was humbling. The life challenges he had faced suddenly seemed insignificant.

Ossia was not quite done telling her story.

"When Edith pass," she said, "I only person at Green House grieve."

Ossia sat quietly, wiped the tears from her cheeks, took a deep breath, and gazed out the window.

A moment later she looked back at Rusty, smiled, and said, "That, Rusty—that my story. Next time, you tell more about you. After that, I explain Edith spirit visit me. Good?"

"Yes Ossia, that sounds good. Thank you for sharing so much. Next time I will tell you about my life."

An Observer

A silent observer had carefully watched and listened to Rusty and Ossia's entire conversation. Standing in the corner of Ossia's room, the observer had paid close attention to each statement Rusty had made and to each reaction he had given to Ossia during the visit.

After Rusty departed, Ossia turned toward that corner of the room and said, "What you think? He good, no?"

The presence of a grey-haired, dark-eyed older woman became partially visible. The observer moved toward Ossia and as she stepped in front of the room's window, light from behind her continued to flow through her body but one could make out that she wore a dark ankle-length pleated skirt and a delicate white silk blouse.

With a gentle French accent, the apparition said, "I think he is kind, Ossia. I like that he is honest and sincere and that he does not appear to be ignorant. You have discovered a friend worth having."

Then the ghost smiled and added, "Such a shame he is so young."

Ossia giggled.

The observer crossed the room. After appearing to sit down on the settee, she added, "I like the portrait you are painting, Ossia. You see into this young man quite well. But perhaps your composition requires more energy—maybe add birds and a tree next to him? And Ossia, his face needs more definition. You must give him a clarity of purpose. Better define the look on his face and in so doing, show your viewer what is in the young man's heart."

Ossia, who had crossed the room to her tea kettle, placed a tea bag into her pink mug. Then she looked back at the portrait for a moment and responded, "Yes, colorful birds, apple tree, good idea. And face definition—yes. You right. Yes, portrait need these."

Ossia poured hot water from the tea kettle into her mug, turned toward her visitor (who happened to be the ghost of Edith Beaulieu), and said, "Yes, Edith, Green House fortunate. Rusty good addition."

A Third Sitting

Two weeks later, Rusty was again sitting on Ossia's stool, sipping tea. Ossia continued to work on his portrait. She was painting the background sky a pale blue, adding dark clouds, and filling in the sketch of the two birds—making one orange and the other red.

Ossia said, "Rusty, today you speak your life."

Rusty took a sip of tea, then replied, "Talking about my life makes me feel uncomfortable, Ossia. I haven't done it that much. In fact, I don't know if anyone has ever asked me to tell them about myself—except, of course, Ann Arbor's prosecuting attorney and the prison's psychologist."

He laughed nervously and said, "Most of when I was young, it was just my mom and me. So, it makes sense for me to tell you a little about her as an introduction to telling you about myself. My mom's life was awfully hard. She grew up on a small farm in Oklahoma and had to work hard around the home. The thing that gave her special pleasure was school and being a good student. Mom often told me how proud she was to graduate from high school. She was the first person in her family to do that and her dream was to go to college. That was in the early years of the Depression and college didn't pan out. What happened instead is that she got pregnant a few months after she finished high school. She went to stay with her aunt in Sheboygan Falls until the baby was born."

Rusty took a deep breath and slowly let the air out before continuing. "That baby was me. Mom never told me much of anything about my birth father. The only time I remember her saying anything about him was when I was about fourteen. Out of the clear blue, Mom made me promise I would never become the sort of dishonest person my father had been. And she never mentioned him again—not once."

It was quiet in the room except for the delicate sound of brush strokes upon canvas as Ossia continued to add color to the portrait.

A few minutes later, while Ossia added yellows and reds to the apples on the tree, Rusty quietly continued. "Mom never went back to Oklahoma. She stayed in Sheboygan Falls and got married when I was a couple of years old. My stepdad taught agriculture at Sheboygan Falls High School. He always treated me nicely. When I was seven or eight, he had to go off to fight in the war."

Rusty paused, then said, "So, it was just Mom and me again. Mom supported us by working in some government office. Mom always treated me gently; gave me lots of love; told me that I was the greatest blessing in her life and how proud she was of my good school grades. She wanted me to go to college."

Ossia interjected, "Rusty, please sit more straight."

Rusty straightened his back.

Ossia said, "Thank you. That better."

Rusty had a thoughtful look on his face as he said. "Mom had only one major vice. She was a smoker. A few months after I graduated from high school, she paid the price. She died from consumption. I had been working part-time as an electrician's apprentice in Grand Rapids and had started taking a few courses at the junior college there. After Mom passed away, I had to quit college and get a full-time job. I worked at a machine shop. During the next couple of years, I paid off all our bills. Then I moved to Ann Arbor. I had been accepted at the university there. I wanted to become a teacher like my stepdad."

Rusty took a sip of tea. After a deep breath and a sigh, he continued. "That was when I screwed everything up. Ann Arbor was an expensive place to live. In addition to the cost of tuition and books, I would have to pay for living expenses. I decided to take a shortcut to get those funds. That was a mistake which I had to pay dearly. Instead of studying whatever at the University of Michigan, I ended up serving time in the state prison. I'd rather not talk about that so much—not right now, anyway. Maybe I'll tell you more about that whole experience some other time. But I'm just not up to it now."

Rusty gave a sad smile and added, "In any case, my life hasn't gone according to any sort of brilliant plan. But I've not experienced the horror you lived through."

Ossia continued to paint.

There was a half an hour silence before Rusty said, "Well, I got to go shopping for some groceries. Maybe we should break now and get together to work on the portrait again soon."

Together at Tony's

Over the next few weeks, the portrait progressed as did the conversation between Ossia and Rusty.

One Saturday morning, as Ossia was mixing colors on her palate, Rusty said, "When I told Tex you were painting my portrait, he made some comment about how you must like me more than him. I didn't know you guys even knew one another. What's the story?"

Ossia giggled.

"That complicated," she said. "I live at Green House long before Tex arrive. Six, maybe seven, years ago, Tex take room. One sunny morning, I return grocery shopping. Tex stand front of Green House. He drunk; tell me he forget key; ask I let him in. I not know him; see he drunk; say, *no*. Open door; go into Green House; close door—all quick. Tex angry. Yell crude words. Ever since, Tex not say word me. I return favor."

She laughed and added, "Problem for Tex? Maybe? Maybe time for him get over. Then no problem."

Rusty chuckled and said, "Sound's fair enough to me."

*****

Life was good. Work was going well and Rusty was enjoying getting to know his housemates.

John and Rusty had formed a modest friendship. Occasionally, they would go to a tavern, have a beer, and watch a Tigers baseball game on the tavern TV. John was always interesting. But Rusty had not lost sight of the fact that John was also unpredictable.

Rusty continued to enjoy the Saturday evenings with Tex and John at Tony's bar. He decided he would try to get Ossia included in these get-togethers. He put the suggestion first to Tex, then to Ossia. Each made clear they had no problem with the idea. It was the other person who had issues.

Once Tex had agreed that Rusty could invite Ossia to join them for the following Saturday evening, Rusty approached John. His concern was that John would find a way to ruin the plan to include Ossia.

John's response to Rusty's suggestion was, "Me? I think it would be great if Ossia joined us. You're the one who has got to talk Tex and Ossia into it."

After Rusty expressed relief sharing that John would not interfere, John said, "Why would anyone ever worry about me causing trouble—on anything—ever?"

Rusty rolled his eyes and John laughed.

"OK," John laughed as he said. "OK. I pledge I will not be an asshole—at least not for that one evening."
*****

The following Saturday evening, Rusty, Tex, John, and Ossia walked over to Tony's Bar together; chattering and laughing the entire way.

A Grosse Point Home

Ten miles east of the Green House, on the outskirts of the prestigious suburb of Grosse Point, was a large white brick home. On this particular day, a fire-engine red Cadillac Eldorado Biarritz convertible was parked on the home's cobblestone driveway. The owner of both the home and the automobile was a sixty-year-old General Motors corporate executive.

If you explored the house, you'd be struck by its red cherry hardwood floors, its dark blue Persian carpets, the home's classic crystal chandeliers, perfectly restored antique furniture and the series of unusual oil paintings hanging throughout the home.

*****

It was 7:30 in the evening. Harry Silva, the home's mildly overweight owner was wearing a royal blue smoker's jacket as he sat on a brown-leather wingback chair in the home's first-floor study. Next to him on a matching chair, was a younger man. Silva's visitor had carefully combed hair and wore a thin-lapeled, grey sharkskin suit with a narrow black tie. The two men smoked large cigars while they sipped whiskey from heavy-weight cut crystal glasses.

"Rank and file won't be happy with this," said the guest.

"Fuck 'em," said Silva. "We gotta be tough, Dan. Union leadership has already received its pound of flesh. The deal is as good as done."

"Of course, you're right, sir," said Silva's visitor.

The two men stood up and shook hands.

The younger man was about to leave when he said, "Before I go, Mr. Silva, my wife CloAnn asked me to check out your art collection. She said she'd heard it's pretty special. My ass will be in a sling if I don't ask to see the art and report back to her."

"She probably heard about the art from my ex-wife," Silva replied while looking down and shaking his head from side to side. "That woman couldn't keep her mouth shut if her life depended on it. She not only gabbed about all of the paintings to me but obviously, to everyone else she met. I'll show you around but I don't know a whole hell of a lot about art."

They started in the living room. Above the fireplace was a colorful still-life of a blue vase full of orange and yellow flowers surrounded by butterflies, bluebirds, and black musical notes.

"Most of these pictures," said Silva, "were painted by the lady who lived here before my dad got the place. That's one of 'em. It's strange. A guy who knows a lot about art once told me he liked the painting. But to me? It just seems weird."

Across from the fireplace above a yellow sofa were four framed, delicately lined ink drawings, two of old men and two of old women.

"Those drawings above the couch are the only art I bought for this place. A worker at the plant who'd served in Italy brought them back after the war. I didn't want to throw my money away on 'em. But my second wife told me I was nuts when I was about to turn 'em down. For once she was right. I found out before the divorce that they're more than three hundred years old and worth a tidy sum." He chuckled and added, "Of course, I hung on to them in the settlement."

The primary interior wall in the dining room had a large painting of two laughing children dancing in a colorful flower garden. In its center, flying above the kids, were two orange and yellow cupids.

"One more weird picture by the original owner's wife," he said. "She must've been awfully strange—I mean, these pictures are right out of the Twilight Zone."

As they walked toward the home's central stairway, Silva's visitor noted, "This house is amazing. How long have you owned it?

"My dad bought it in 1930. The stooge who lived here jumped out of an office window—on black Tuesday. After his wife couldn't pay her husband's debts, the bank foreclosed and my dad grabbed it. He rented it out for almost a decade before I asked him to give it to me and my first wife as a wedding present. That was in '38, right after I started at GM. My wife tried to hang onto the house in the divorce. There was no fucking way I was going to let that happen. My dad once gave me some important practical advice: *The spouse with the best attorney always wins.* I've never ignored that principle."

As they walked up the grand staircase, Silva said, "After my dad gave me the place, all I did was have its exterior painted and a few pieces of furniture refinished. Still, after being rented out for almost a decade, the place was in pretty decent shape. Most of the paintings you see were done by the widow of that guy who killed himself. Her work has become pretty valuable. A couple of years ago, some art dealer showed up at my door and offered me nine thousand bucks for the dining room painting—nine thousand fucking bucks for that odd painting of the flowers and those little gremlins! Can you believe it? That was a whole hell of a lot more than my dad paid for the place when he got it in 1930."

Harry Silva led his visitor up a grand staircase.

Midway, he stopped on the staircase's landing and studied a large oil painting. "This painting always throws me for a loop," he said. "It's supposed to be valuable as well. But what the hell do two naked middle-aged women standing together, holding hands while they float in the sky have to do with anything? And that full moon next to them with the ring of flowers: What the hell is that supposed to mean? The painting is totally weird."

Silva shook his head and began walking up the stairs. He stopped, turned to his visitor, and said, "Now I have a favor to ask of you, Dan. I know you promised your CloAnn that you'd tell her about the art. But in describing the place, don't make it sound special. Just tell her you looked at the art and there wasn't anything so impressive. And if you would, suggest she not speak with others about the paintings. Tell her I like my privacy. I'd appreciate that a lot, Dan. While I have an alarm system, I don't need anyone getting ambitious and trying to rip me off. So, if you'd just tell her that, I'd be indebted to you. I'm sure there'll come a day when I can return the favor."

His visitor said, "Sure, Mr. Silva. Absolutely."

As they walked down the grand staircase to the front door, Silva said, "Thank you for your help on our, uhm, project—and also, for your discretion regarding my privacy. By the way, Dan, in the future, go ahead and call me Harry."

The visitor struggled to suppress a smile while saying, "Sure thing, Harry."

The two men shook hands and Dan, a grin on his face, was out the door.

Tuesday in October

It was a cold, windy Tuesday afternoon in October. Inside the Green House, it was warm. Ossia sat on her red velvet chair drinking a cup of mint tea with honey. On the settee next to her was the apparition of her dear friend, Edith Beaulieu.

"Tell about painting again, Edith," said Ossia. "Describe it again. Each time you describe, I appreciate more."

Edith smiled and said, "I painted that amazing image after awakening from an enchanted dream. Despite its beauty, the image somehow made me sad. Those two women standing together—in the sky. I didn't know who they were, Ossia. I just knew I needed to paint them. Maybe one of them—the one looking down with a rose in her hand—maybe that was me. The other woman? I don't know who she was, only that she was important to deciphering the vision. In the dream—and in the painting—there were no stars in the sky. But there was a full moon surrounded by a ring of yellow dahlias and white lilacs."

Ossia took a sip of tea while she watched Edith gaze out the window.

Edith turned toward her and said, "Those two women, they were holding hands. You could see they had been weeping. And behind them, across the horizon, below that dark sky, were fluffy yellow and pink clouds. That image held a magical story that I never have been able to interpret—only to appreciate. I have always wondered about it. When I awoke, Ossia, I knew it was important to paint it. I only wish I could take you to my elegant home to show you that composition—and all my other creations."

Edith looked off across the room and out the window before saying, "That is if my paintings are still in the house. I think they must be—they have to be. My agent Carl Black told me—before I passed, that the home's owners had not sold my artwork, that my works remain where I hung them."

Edith Beaulieu added, "I miss them so much, Ossia. They were like my children. I miss them so much."

There was silence in the room. With a resolute look, Ossia turned to Edith and said, "I ask Rusty, John, and Tex go visit. They find way confirm paintings still in house."

Making a Plan

The following Saturday evening was the third time Ossia joined Tex, John, and Rusty at Tony's bar. John and Rusty split the cost of a second pizza so that the four housemates could eat their fill.

Tex had just completed his second set closing out with a slide guitar interpretation of *Blue Suede Shoes*. He returned to his housemates' table with a smile on his face. As the cheering and clapping from the bar's patrons subsided, he sat down, poured himself a beer, and took a long drink.

That was when Ossia asked Tex, John, and Rusty if they would do her a favor. After several pitchers of beer, the men were feeling gallant. John spoke for the others when he assured Ossia that her wish was their command.

"Edith Beaulieu explain me about wonderful home she call the *White House*. She say she believe her paintings still hang in home—she not certain. She ask us visit home in Grosse Point, look in window, see if paintings there."

The men were slightly inebriated and in a daring state of mind.

Tex said, "Sure. That'd be a piece of cake, Ossia. You got the address?"

"Edith give me," responded Ossia as she placed a small piece of paper onto the table. An address was handwritten on it.

John took the paper, placed it in his wallet, and said, "First off, I'll go to Grosse Point's City Hall and figure out who currently lives in the house. Then I'll drive by and check it out. After that, Tex, Rusty, and I can go there and look in the windows. Who knows, maybe we can even figure out a way to get into the house and see the paintings—eh Rusty?"

Rusty glared at John and didn't respond.

Tex said, "OK. I like the plan."

A few minutes later, Rusty changed the topic by complimenting Tex on his rendition of *Blue Suede Shoes*. That led to an animated debate between John and Tex regarding whether Elvis Presley's music fit into the country or the rock and roll genre. Rusty and Ossia just watched as Tex and John went at it.

Half an hour later, the four housemates trudged home through a cold rain driven by a biting October wind.

As they opened the door to the Green House, Ossia thanked the men for promising to visit Edith Beaulieu's home and asked, "When you go?"

John responded, "Let's target next week. Rusty, maybe you could ride along with me when I do my drive-by?"

Rusty gave another dirty look at John before saying, "OK."

A Trip to Grosse Point

Wednesday, Rusty took a vacation day from work.

At ten that morning, John pulled up in front of the Green House in his shiny red and white '59 Chevy Impala coupe. The car's windows were down and John was slouching behind the steering wheel listening to WXYZ-AM 1270 playing Patsy Cline's hit, "She's Got You".

"Pretty classy wheels," Rusty said as he got into the front passenger seat.

"Yup. She's got a 283 cubic inch V8 in her," said John. "This baby's got more power than I know what to do with."

John put his *baby* into drive and pulled into light traffic. He turned the radio even louder when the station began to play Jerry Lee Lewis's "Great Balls of Fire." A half an hour later, John pulled the Chevy over to the side of the road and took out a map. Rusty sat waiting, listening to the radio as WXYZ continued to put out a mix of country-western and rock-and-roll hits.

After studying the map for a few minutes, John said, "Good. I know how to get there, now." He pulled into the light traffic and soon they were in an upscale community of beautifully landscaped yards and imposing homes. A moment later, he pulled the sleek Chevy over to the curb and turned off the ignition. Lake St Claire was on their right and a large white brick house was on their left.

"That's it, Rusty. I went to Grosse Pointe's city hall yesterday and spoke with a clerk. I finagled the name of the guy who lives here out of him. The name's Harry Silva. The clerk said he is a manager at GM's Clark Street Cadillac Assembly Plant. That's where Tex works."

The two men sat in the shiny red car for half an hour with their eyes glued on the big white house, looking for any sign of activity within it.

"Yesterday afternoon," said John, "I went up to speak with Tex after he returned from work. I told him who owns the house. Tex told me Silva's a son of a bitch. He's the head honcho there and the workers hate him. He told me Silva's not married. So, if he's at work, there's probably no one home. Tex and I talked a little bit about whether you could figure out how to get us in there."

Rusty gave John a dirty look and said, "Yeah, where is this going?"

John turned to Rusty and said, "I haven't told you everything."

OK, Rusty thought to himself. *Here it comes. John is about to screw me.*

John kept talking. "After I found out about your time in the joint at the Michigan Department of Corrections, I wondered what kind of burglaries you might have pulled off in Ann Arbor. I went to the library and read a few old issues of the *Ann Arbor News*. I was looking for stories about your break-ins."

Rusty glared at John who looked away and didn't stop speaking. "I learned you were quite discriminating in selecting the homes you chose to rob. The *News* referred to you as *a skilled thief* and described how capable you were at picking locks. It also reviewed your knowledge of alarm systems. I know I didn't mention this when I admitted I'd butted into your business. But I'll give you my word, I haven't said anything to anybody about what I learned."

Rusty quietly said, "Yeah, your word, John—that seems to be worth a whole hell of a lot."

John finished up. "When this whole thing came up about getting into Edith Beaulieu's house, I realized you were the perfect—how shall I say it—partner in crime. I'm telling you this now because I know you can get us into this big old white palace."

John had looked away from Rusty throughout his admission.

Then he looked back at Rusty and said, "Anyway, let's go pound on the door and find out if anyone's home. If someone answers, I'll tell them that we're with, uhm—."

John paused for a moment before saying, "I'll tell them that we're preaching the savior's word. If I do that, they will let us get out of there in an instant."

After John got out of the car, he walked up the cobblestone walkway to the house. At first, Rusty stayed in the car watching John approach the home. Then he shook his head with a look of disgust, got out of the Impala, and followed John up the walk.

At the door, Rusty whispered to John, "I have no clue why I was the one who ended up in prison instead of you."

John ignored Rusty's comment as he pressed an elegant brass doorbell button which had *The Silvas* printed above it in golden script. The two men listened to a short rendition of "Westminster Chimes." When no one came to the door, John pressed the doorbell again. They listened to an encore of the chimes. Again, there was no response.

John turned and walked on a stone walkway that led around the north side of the home. He looked back over his shoulder at Rusty and whispered, "Let's check out the backyard."

Rusty watched, unsure whether he should follow.

John, who had made his way around the corner of the house, returned to where Rusty could see him and said, "Rusty, check this out. It's some sort of alarm system."

Rusty's curiosity had been teased. He followed John around the corner and saw him gazing at a small grey metal box on the side of the home. Printed on the slightly rusted box in black ink was *ADEMCO Deluxe Combination Burglar Fire Alarm*. Above the box was a grey, rusted six-inch-wide alarm bell.

John said, "Let's try to find a window that will allow us to look inside the house."

Then he opened the picket fence gate which led to the backyard. Suddenly, a large German Shepherd rushed at John, showing his teeth and barking loudly. John reached inside his jacket pocket and produced a large dog biscuit. He held the tan bone-shaped treat out to the dog. When the German Shepherd reached John, instead of attacking him, he took the biscuit from John's hand and started wagging his tail. John had made a friend.

John laughed and said, "I read an article that said if you are snooping around someone's home, always carry a few dog treats. The article said mailmen often carry dog biscuits for situations just like this."

John and Rusty, accompanied by the happy, tail-wagging dog, walked into the backyard. There, past the patio and behind a neatly trimmed laurel hedge, they saw a pair of large picture windows. John slid behind the bushes and looked into the house. Rusty followed.

Through one of the windows, they could see into the dining room. There was a fancy dining table and chairs with a large chandelier hanging over it. Behind it was a matching buffet. Hung above the buffet was a large painting of some kids in a flower garden that had two angels above the kids.

The next window allowed John and Rusty to view the house's grand living room. It had an ornate oriental carpet with an impressive set of antique furniture. On its walls were several old master-type portrait drawings. Above the fireplace was a large, colorful painting depicting a vase of flowers that was surrounded by an arrangement of butterflies, bluebirds, and large black musical notes.

John chuckled and said, "Well, Rusty. Those two big paintings are awfully damn strange. They almost seem like things Ossia might have painted. Now that we've scouted the place out, we should probably get out of Dodge."

As they turned around, John gave the big drooling dog a second biscuit. He patted the happy German Shepherd's head for a few seconds. Then the two men retraced their steps, carefully shutting the gate, and headed back to John's Impala.

*****

Ten minutes later, as John drove back toward their home, he turned on the radio which was playing "The Battle of New Orleans." Both men laughed as they listened to Johnny Horton sing:

Yeah, they ran through the briars and they ran through the brambles
And they ran through the bushes where a rabbit couldn't go.
They ran so fast that the hounds couldn't catch 'em
Down the Mississippi to the Gulf of Mexico.

After listening to the final chorus of the song, John said, "If Andrew Jackson had had some dog biscuits, he would not have had to run through the brambles and the bushes."

Rusty's silent response to John's joke was to roll his eyes.

John turned off the radio and said, "That living room sure looked cool. I wonder what the rest of the place was like."

"Maybe the living room was cool," said Rusty, "but if someone had shown up, if they had called the police, we might have ended up cooling our chops in Grosse Point's city jail."

Rusty paused, then added, "And I might have ended up with my parole revoked—and been sent back to the state prison."

"I understand, Rusty. Sorry to put you in that spot."

"Sure, John. You sound really sorry—almost as if you fucking cared."

They rode the rest of the way back to the Green House in silence.

*****

After Tex returned from his shift at the Clark Street Assembly Plant, John and Rusty went to Tex's room to update him on their visit to Edith Beaulieu's old home. John reviewed all they had seen. Rusty said nothing.

Tex listened, then said, "Silva's a son of a bitch. He screws us every chance he gets. Nobody—and I include the plant's supervisors—not anyone there likes the creep. Anytime there's any kind of conflict on the assembly line, Silva fires somebody. He particularly likes to go after colored workers."

There was quiet in the room for a minute.

Then Tex said, "Tell Ossia about what you saw. Hear her thoughts. I think that since the home's protected by an alarm system, we should forget about it."

John gave a tentative glance at Rusty, then said, "I'm not saying we have to go in there. But the alarm system—it shouldn't stop us. We've got a master thief here. I'm willing to bet he knows exactly how to turn that system off."

Rusty scowled and said, "John, you're a royal asshole."

Tex asked, "What do you mean, John—*turn the system off?*"

Rusty interrupted. "John's full of shit. I'm not going to get manipulated into doing any breaking and entering. I don't give a flying fuck how simple that alarm system is. You guys get caught in that little castle, you'll innocently tell the judge you were just fooling around and get off with a warning. Me? I get sent back for a few more years to the state pen. John—this is bullshit. You are about as trustworthy as a rattlesnake."

Tex ignored Rusty's statement and asked, "What do you mean, the system's simple. How do you know that?"

"During high school, I worked part-time for an electrician. The guy's specialty was installing alarm systems. He had some pretty rich clients. Oftentimes, he would just tell me what to do, and I'd end up installing the whole damn alarm system."

Tex and John glanced at one another, then turned back to Rusty waiting to hear anything else Rusty would say.

Rusty took a breath and sighed. Then he said, "A couple of years after I graduated from high school, I got accepted into the University of Michigan. I moved to Ann

Arbor. My plan was to work my way through school. Except I couldn't find anything that paid more than minimum wage and that wouldn't cover my living, tuition, and book costs. I saw the fancy homes in Ann Arbor and decided to relieve a few of their owners of some jewelry and other valuables as a means of funding my education."

Rusty walked over to the window and gazed out in silence. Then he shook his head sadly, turned to the others, and said, "I scouted out the larger homes in prestigious Ann Arbor neighborhoods on Saturdays when Michigan had home football games. Alarms are often mounted outside homes near where the electricity and phone wire hook-ups are found. Checking that area on candidate homes led me to some with alarm systems like the ones I'd installed. My theory was that if a place had an alarm system, its owner had some valuable shit inside. Once I identified a target, I'd watch it on game days. If I saw a homeowner take off, I would ring the doorbell. If no one answered, I'd go around the home, silence the alarm system, and select a window I could easily open as my entry point. Then I would do my shopping, so to speak. I sold the stuff I ripped off at a pawn shop in Detroit, banked the proceeds, and planned on ending the break-ins and attending classes during winter term."

Rusty grimaced before saying, "Unfortunately, the cops had been keeping an eye on that pawn shop. They spotted some stuff I'd stolen there and I got ratted out by the pawnbroker. Bottom line, trying to take shortcuts to move my life forward ended up setting me back. I got arrested, tried in court, and sent directly to jail. I did not pass *go* nor did I *collect two hundred dollars*. The whole thing was a big dumb screw-up. What I am trying to do now is fix my life and move it forward."

The only sound in the Tex's room was now coming from the street whenever an occasional automobile passed. Rusty's voice had become quieter and quieter as he spoke. Now, almost in a whisper, he said, "Then my pal John decides he wants to play Sherlock Holmes. After he confessed this morning to having dug into my past, he gave me his solemn word he would never mention anything about my crimes to anyone—not ever."

Rusty scowled. "That lasted about five hours. John, your promises are good for nothing. Sure. I could pick the lock and get into the alarm system box. All I would need to do would be to open it up and detach a couple of wires. It would be disarmed. But I'll be damned, Tex, if I am going to go through that again. End of story. I already screwed up my life once by breaking into homes and I am not into repeating my mistakes. If that weren't reason enough, I just don't trust John. I will never work with this liar on any task that has risk associated with it."

Tex said to Rusty. "Sorry, man. Thanks for explaining."

Then Tex looked at John and said, "Way to screw it up, asshole."

*****

Rusty returned to his room while John and Tex went down to update Ossia on the morning's visit to Grosse Point.

Later that evening, Tex told Rusty about that visit with Ossia. "John described your trip to Grosse Point without mentioning your background with alarm systems. I talked about what a creep Silva is. I told Ossia that going into the home wasn't worth the risk. I added that you felt the same way about it. When I stopped speaking, Ossia asked why you hadn't joined us in updating her. I just said that you didn't feel the whole thing was worth the risk and didn't want to be a part of it in any way."

"What did she say?" asked Rusty

Tex responded, "Ossia told me she understood. Then she said she needed to consult with Edith. After that, we left and that was the end of it."

Ossia's Next Conversation

After Tex and John left her room, Ossia walked over to her easel, lifted the cloth off of the portrait of Rusty, and began to carefully touch up the dark shadows under Rusty's eyes.

A voice from behind Ossia said, "The portrait looks nice. It's almost complete."

"Yes, Edith," said Ossia. "Rusty spirit well captured. Show him portrait now—agree?"

Edith replied, "Yes, I think so. He will appreciate it."

There was silence in the room as Ossia continued to touch up details on the canvas.

"When Tex and John visited you today," said Edith, "they did not share everything that was said when they met with Rusty."

Ossia replied, "What you say?"

The semi-transparent illusion of a gray-haired woman wearing a cable knit sweater and dark slacks appeared. Edith's ghost gave a piercing look into Ossia's eyes as she said, "Today, when John and Rusty met with Tex, John told Tex that there is a burglar alarm system in the White House. He explained that an alarm system should not interfere with their entry because Rusty has expertise in alarm systems. Ossia, we both know John is a terrible busybody. However, on this occasion, that may offer some value. John researched Rusty's crimes. He discovered that the reason Rusty was sent to prison was that he had broken into homes. But what is relevant here is that Rusty knows how to turn off a house's alarm system."

The ghost of Edith watched Ossia stop painting and put down her paintbrush.

Ossia asked, "Why they not say?"

Edith turned her head at an angle and gave a shrewd look. "Rusty was furious that John had pried into his past. He became even more angry because John had told someone else about his crimes. Rusty told Tex and John that he will never break into a home again. He fears being arrested and placed, once again, into a prison. Still, Ossia— what's important here is that Rusty knows how to turn off the White House's alarm system. With Rusty's skills, John and Tex could enter my wonderful home."

And having said that, Edith's image faded away.

After Edith had disappeared, Ossia stood in front of the portrait for five minutes, gazing at the image she had created of Rusty. She walked over to her still-hot tea kettle, poured hot water into her cup, and returned to the portrait. She looked at the almost complete canvas for several minutes before she picked up a thin liner paint brush, dabbed it in black paint, and carefully continued to highlight Rusty's eyes.

*****

The following evening, there was a knock on Ossia's door. She opened it and saw Rusty.

"So nice you visit. Teapot full and fresh. You want cup delicious hibiscus tea?"

"That would be nice, Ossia."

Ossia went to her kitchenette as Rusty made his way to the settee and took a seat.

"This evening," she said from across the room, "I show portrait. It complete."

Ossia walked over to Rusty, put two mugs of tea down on the coffee table, and walked over to her easel. After turning the easel so that Rusty would be able to see the painting, she pulled back the cloth and revealed the portrait.

The painting's foreground showed Rusty's head and shoulders. In the composition, he had a thoughtful expression. Next to him was an apple tree and on its branches, in addition to several colorful apples, were two birds. One was orange and the other red. The portrait's background was a violet and pink sky. In its upper corner, above the apple tree, was a dark threatening cloud. A single lightning bolt emerged from that cloud.

"Portrait, my gift to you, Rusty. I hope you like."

Rusty's face turned red as he said, "No. Ossia. I can't accept this. It's–it's just too extraordinary. It's too generous."

"You must accept, Rusty. Gift given. Saying *no* steal my joy in giving. We not discuss more. When you leave chamber this evening, you carry portrait."

Rusty took a moment to respond. In a choked-up voice, he said, "This is the nicest gift anyone has ever given to me. I am humbled—completely humbled. Thank you so much."

Ossia beamed and returned to her chair. The two friends silently sipped tea.

Ten minutes of silence later, Rusty said, "I have a question I need to ask."

"Please ask."

"Did you get a visit from Tex and John yesterday?"

"Yes."

"Could you tell me about it?"

Ossia described the visit, accurately recounting everything shared with her by the two men.

Then she added, "I know more, Rusty. After John, Tex leave, have other visitor. Learn more story."

Rusty gave a confused look.

"John and Tex leave," she said. "I continue paint. Ghost my friend Edith visit me. Edith able visit all rooms in Green House. This way, she hear many conversations. Edith explain me, John and Tex not say everything. She explain they promise you say nothing about house alarm knowledge of you. She say you able turn off alarm systems. Tell you go into Ann Arbor houses—take things. Edith say you refuse go into White House because you fear prison. I understand. So many years, I locked in rooms."

Rusty was speechless. He had been told Ossia believed she could talk to a ghost. Rusty hadn't thought much about that because he felt she was a little off her rocker. Now, he had to either accept that she had spoken with a ghost or believe that Tex and John had not kept their promise. Rusty sat stone-faced and silent while he considered his dilemma. Ossia quietly waited. Finally, Rusty concluded that the idea of a ghost spying on him was just too far out there.

"Ossia," he said, "I don't believe in ghosts. I'm sorry. I have to think about this whole thing. I appreciate the tea and the company. But I need to take some time to work my way through all of this. I'm sorry. I just don't believe in ghosts."

He stood up and without saying another word or taking the painting that had, moments before, been so graciously given to him, Rusty left Ossia's room.

*****

The following Saturday evening, Tex performed his regular act at Tony's. Between sets, he sat at his table by himself. John wasn't welcome. Ossia was devastated by what had transpired between her and Rusty. And Rusty? He wouldn't speak with anyone living in the Green House.

Winter Arrives

The seasons changed. The brisk breeze of October turned into the cold sharp wind of November. Rusty's work at Grace Hospital continued to go well but the pleasure of living in the Green House had vanished. He avoided Tex, John, and Ossia. Each of those housemates had asked him if he would discuss the situation. Rusty gave the same response to each request, "There is just no point in talking."

*****

It was the second week of November—a Friday evening. As Rusty returned from work, he saw Jeannine standing in the hall outside her apartment. She asked him to come inside to speak with her.

While Rusty's voice said, "Of course Jeannine," his mind was telling him, *John ratted me out. He fucked me over one last time. I'm about to be told that since I lied when I took the room, I will have to find another place to live.*

Rusty had never been inside Jeannine's apartment. He was surprised with the amount of space in her main room. On the streetside, Jeannine had a small couch, a coffee table, and two red upholstered chairs. Across the room by her kitchenette, was a small dining table and two chairs. The chairs were similar to the ones by the couch.

"I see from your expression you are surprised by my apartment. When Edith Beaulieu moved into the Green House, she combined rooms 101 and 103 into one apartment. She made the back room smaller and used it as her painting studio. I use it as a bedroom. The larger room is my salon. Please take a seat," Jeannine said pointing to the couch. "There's something we need to discuss. However first," she said, "can I offer you a glass of wine?"

"Yes," Rusty responded, "a glass of wine would be nice."

Rusty had prepared himself to have Jeannine kick him out of the house. Now, he was taken aback. Why had she offered him a glass of wine if she was about to throw him out on the street?

A few minutes later, Jeannine placed two crystal wine glasses and a carafe of red wine on the coffee table. She sat down across from him and filled each of the glasses. After Rusty had taken a taste, his wide-eyed expression must have communicated that he recognized the exceptional quality of the wine she had served.

Jeannine spoke to Rusty in French. *"Je vois à votre expression que vous appréciez un bon Bordeaux."*

"Merci," he responded. *"Ce vin est incroyable, Madame."*

She smiled and said, "When you first rented the room, I did not miss your skill with the French language. We will not speak French today even though I appreciate how well you speak the language of my homeland."

She paused as she tasted the Bordeaux.

"This *is* an exceptional vintage," she said. "But no, I didn't invite you in to discuss wine either. Ever since you moved into this building, Rusty, I have appreciated your thoughtfulness—your respect for your housemates. Yet over the past few weeks, I have seen that you have separated yourself from the others who live here. I watched this but did not interfere. I know that it is not my place to meddle in boarders' lives."

Jeannine took another sip and closed her eyes as she savored the wine's taste.

"However," she said, "this conversation is an exception to that rule. The residents of the Green House come from different backgrounds, have had different life experiences and have unique personalities. To illustrate, I have not missed how thoughtless John can be. He is not a bad person—just someone who sometimes is tedious and often a little confused. Tex? I do not know him well. We never have had a personal conversation. Yet, I see what a good person he is—such an honest man—always kind to all who live here."

Rusty continued to listen without saying anything. He was worried where this was going.

"Ossia? She is my favorite. Ossia has faced so much brutality and so many unfair life challenges. I am not sure how she survived—not at all. Yet she has survived and has found peace here in the Green House. Ossia brings with her a tranquility that has benefited others."

Jeannine's look became grave.

Here it comes, Rusty thought to himself.

"Yesterday," Jeannine said, "I learned what happened between you and your friends—the whole story. I learned that you and John visited the home of my Aunt Edith. After that, the two of you updated Tex. Then Tex and John went to Ossia's room to brief her. However, your impression of what occurred there is incorrect. John and Tex revealed no secrets about your past—things they had promised to keep secret."

Jeannine paused. She took a sip of wine, then said, "After they left Ossia's room, the ghost of my Aunt Edith visited Ossia. Edith shared with Ossia what she had heard when John and you met with Tex earlier in the evening. Edith told Ossia all about the home robberies you committed in Ann Arbor and about your knowledge of home alarm systems."

Rusty's mind was reeling. He felt for a moment, like he was Alice in Wonderland—not certain in any way of what he would be presented with next. He leaned forward, paying close attention to each word spoken by Jeannine.

"Yes, Rusty," Jeannine continued, "there is a ghost in the Green House. My Aunt Edith haunts this building. Occasionally, she even visits me. But her favorite person is Ossia. Last night, Edith did visit me. She shared all of those things that I just repeated to you. She also suggested—no, she directed me to speak with you."

Rusty was in a mild state of shock. He waited for whatever would come next. The silence in Jeannine's apartment became almost deafening.

As Jeannine paused, she took a deep breath, then said, "I understand that John showed utter contempt for you by digging into your past. That was horrid, but unfortunately quite typical of John's self-indulgent behavior. When Ossia shared with you what Edith had told her, you not only refused to believe what Ossia said, but you refused to accept her gift, the portrait Ossia had painted of you. Shame on you, Rusty. How could you do that? Ossia is such a sweet injured soul. Edith told me how sad Ossia has been ever since that evening. How could you have done that to such an innocent person?"

By now, Rusty was not feeling afraid of being kicked out of the home. He was just plain ashamed of, and embarrassed by, his actions. He sat in silence—not because he felt he would be out on the street if he chose not to believe in a ghost. Rusty felt an overpowering sense of shame for having hurt Ossia.

Jeannine continued. "My aunt Edith directed me—
Fix it, she said. That is what I am trying to do right now. Yes,
Rusty, this house is haunted. It is haunted by a good ghost
who comes to us from across whatever chasm exists between
this life and the next. This good ghost does not want to see
the people for whom she cares hurt. So now, Rusty, I am
saying to you what Edith said to me. Fix it." She paused, then
added, "Will you do that?"

Either everybody else in the building was lying to
him or the ghost of the house's original owner did, in fact,
exist. After considering his options and their consequences,
Rusty chose to suspend his prior disbelief in the
supernatural. He responded to Jeannine by saying, "OK. I'll
fix it."

"Thank you, Rusty. I trust that you will do this well
and quickly. However," Jeannine continued, "something
else is troubling me. I don't know if you are aware that Tex
may have to leave the Green House. Tex's assembly plant
fired his colored friend even though the man had done
nothing wrong. Tex was angry about that injustice. He
complained to his union about what had occurred. The next
day, Tex was called into the plant's personnel office and told
that he was being fired. Tex told me that if he can't find
another job, he will have to leave us. He won't be able to pay
the rent."

Rusty was shocked. Tex had befriended him when he
came to the Green House. Now, he was being hit with this!
Life just didn't seem fair.

After Jeannine told Rusty about Tex, she stood up.
Rusty followed suit.

"Thank you, Rusty, for listening to me," she said.
"How you fix things is your business. But you must know

that Tex and John did not deceive you in what they shared with Ossia and Ossia told you the truth about Edith. You were wrong and you inflicted pain on others. In addition, Tex is facing a massive challenge in his life. This is a time in which all of us must be especially respectful of his circumstances."

Rusty, head hanging low, was about to leave when Jeannine added, "I follow a simple rule in life. I do not expect others to be more perfect than myself. We all have done things we regret. I don't care that you were in jail—or why you were there. You are a good person—perhaps a little foolish—but yes, a good person."

Jeannine looked him in the eye and said, "However, young man, now you must go about repairing this situation."

Mending Fences

After Rusty left Jeannine's apartment, he was resting in his room, thinking about the conversation that had just occurred.

"Damn," he said to himself. "I screwed this situation up good."

He took a deep breath, then spoke out loud (though no one was there to hear his words), "Time to go eat some humble pie."

*****

A couple of minutes later, Rusty was knocking on Tex's door.

"Come on in," was Tex's response.

Rusty opened the door. Tex was sitting on his bed in his shorts and undershirt, changing the strings on his Dobro. He looked up at Rusty and simply said, "Yeah?"

"Jeannine pulled me aside this afternoon. She explained what an asshole I've been."

Tex said nothing at first. He just continued to adjust the Dobro guitar's peg and pluck at the string, continuing to finetune the pitch of that one string.

"Okay," Tex said. "She nailed that one. Anything else?"

"I'm apologizing. John's meddling in my backstory got under my skin. I don't trust the guy and I took it out on you and Ossia. I was wrong. I'm sorry."

Tex plucked another string on his guitar and adjusted its peg. For a short while, he continued plucking, adjusting, and plucking. Still not looking up, Tex said, "Apologized to Ossia yet?"

"You're first. Ossia's next. I wanted to start with you. You were the one who welcomed me into the Green House. But I know, I've acted like a jerk. I'll head down to her room right after we speak."

"Yeah," Tex said. "You're right, Rusty. You've been a jerk."

Tex stopped adjusting the guitar and, apparently satisfied, carefully placed the instrument onto his bed.

Then he looked up and said, "Still, I've been known to act like a jerk once or twice myself. With that in mind, I accept your apology. But you need to fix this with Ossia. That little lady didn't do anything to you. What you do with John on the other hand—well, that's your business. I agree. He's a jerk."

"Have you eaten?" Rusty asked.

Tex didn't respond immediately, then gave a tentative reply. "Nope."

"Can I buy you dinner at the Warren Avenue Diner?"

Tex took a moment before responding. "Sure. That'd be fine. We can go in an hour. That'll give you a chance to fix things with Ossia first."

*****

A few minutes later, Rusty was knocking on Ossia's door. The door opened. Ossia stood in front of him.

"Hello," was her empty one-word welcome.

"Can I visit?" Rusty said. "I have some stuff to say beginning with *I owe you an apology*."

"Can come in," Ossia said quietly. She led Rusty to the settee and gestured for him to take a seat. She sat on the chair next to him.

Looking at the floor, not glancing at Rusty's watchful face, Ossia spoke slowly and quietly. "What you say?"

"I'm ashamed of how I've behaved, Ossia," Rusty began. "You welcomed me and made me feel like I belonged here. You told me you were aware I was a thief, something John and Tex had promised not to repeat. You told me Edith—the ghost of Edith, that is—had been the one to tell you. I didn't believe in ghosts. I thought you were lying to me—or worse yet, mocking me. I thought Jeannine would find out about my crimes, that I would get kicked out of the Green House."

Ossia continued to look down at the aged oak floor.

"About an hour ago, Jeannine explained that Edith—well, the ghost of Edith really does exist. Jeannine was gentle with her words, yet quite direct. She told me I had hurt others. She let me know I had been unkind. She told me I needed to fix what I had broken."

Rusty paused, then added, "Jeannine told me about Tex losing his job."

Ossia sighed but said nothing for a couple of minutes. An ominous silence took over the room.

When Ossia looked up, she said in almost a whisper, "Rusty. I know pain. I spend years with pain. You hurt me. Deep."

She paused before adding, "And Tex—he offer you friendship. You slap him—across face. You call honest man liar. How you do that? Tex fear lose job, leave Green House. Yet you call him liar. You hurt Tex."

Ossia's whisper demonstrated an anger that Rusty had not heard from her before. He sat and listened. He knew he deserved the scolding.

She continued. "And John? Maybe John feel nothing. I not care. John is all about John."

Ossia paused, took a deep breath, and said, "Thank you for apology. Tonight, I reflect. Tomorrow, maybe next day, we talk."

Having said that, Ossia stood up and led Rusty to her door.

*****

After Rusty had left her room, Ossia returned to her chair. She slowly sat down, bent her head forward, covered her eyes with her hands, and wept.

From across the room, a voice said, "This is hard, Ossia, awfully hard. I am so sorry."

"Thank you, Edith. So strange. Spirit my only friend. You always kind. Always give love. This important for me. Thank you."

"Oh Ossia, there is so much pain in this world. And I understand you have experienced more than your fair share. I am so sorry. Other folk in the Green House—they also have experienced pain. Pain causes people to do things that don't make sense. Rusty is a good person. He too has received more than his share of pain. Rusty needs a friend—maybe more than you do. That friendship is something you can provide."

Ossia remained quiet. Her eyes continued to focus on the room's old oak floor. When she looked up, she said, "You right, Edith, as always. Thank you. You always the best friend anyone could wish. You are my family."

And once again she bent her head forward into her open hands and wept.

*****

A few minutes later, Rusty lay in bed, thinking about the mess he had created for himself. There was a knock on the door. "Probably Tex ready to go," he thought.

"C'mon in," he said as he pivoted into a sitting position.

It was not Tex. It was Ossia.

"I speak with Edith, Rusty," she said as she stood in the door. "Edith tell me, time forgive. She explain you make mistake. Pain in your life too. So, I say *yes*. Accept apology. Now, you accept portrait."

And as she walked into the room, she handed him the portrait.

"Room need color. I accept apology. Now you accept portrait."

Rusty gave a big smile. "You got yourself a deal, Ossia. Thank you for accepting my apology. And thank you for this wonderful painting. There is one more side to this deal. You have to go to dinner with Tex and me this evening at the Warren Avenue Diner—my treat!"

Ossia gave a panicked look. "I not dressed! How I go like this?"

Rusty gave a wide grin. "Go to your room, Ossia. Get ready. Tex and I'll pick you up in fifteen minutes. It's cold outside. Wear your warm coat."

*****

After Ossia left, Rusty took down the Detroit Tigers 1962 calendar that had been hanging from a nail on the wall above the head of his bed. He hung the portrait on that nail. Then he stood back and admired the painting and smiled. It was a nice portrait and Ossia had been right. His room badly needed some color.

Now he, Rusty Nolan, had an original work of art hanging in his room, providing much-needed color and light.

A Thanksgiving – More or Less

An hour later, Ossia, Tex, and Rusty were sitting in a booth at the Warren Avenue Diner. In front of each of them was an open-faced hot turkey sandwich complete with mashed potatoes, gobs of gravy, overcooked green beans, and cranberries. Tex and Rusty each had a bottle of Budweiser in front of them. Ossia had a white porcelain cup with a Lipton Tea tag hanging off of its side.

After good-naturedly taking a fair amount of teasing from Tex and Ossia about being thin-skinned, Rusty changed the topic by asking, "So what's the story with John?"

Ossia and Tex look at one another.

Tex responded. "I think the chaos that followed your temper tantrum upset John more than anyone else. At first, he tried to blame everything on you. I ripped him a new asshole on that one. A couple of days later, he agreed he was the one who had screwed everything up. It was good to see John humbled a bit after he had been such an ass.

Ossia added, "Agree. John the problem. Shame on him."

"Actually," Tex added, "the only good thing to come out of your temper tantrum was John's figuring out that if he hadn't been such a snoop, there'd never have been a problem."

"I can't let him take all of the credit," said Rusty with a chuckle. "Just most of it."

The friends laughed.

Ossia offered, "I not speak John for weeks. That not good."

Rusty replied, "I guess that's my department. I'll have to speak with John next."

"Lucky guy," quipped Tex.

Rusty turned toward Tex and said, "Jeannine told me you'd been fired. That true?"

Tex spun his Budweiser bottle back and forth between his right thumb and pointer finger. Then he looked down at the table and replied, "Yup, Rusty. I got the old pink slip a couple of weeks ago."

After Tex looked up, he added, "The guy whose house you and John checked out, Silva—he's chief honcho at the plant where I work—he's the person behind my getting fired. Everyone at Clark Street knows Silva's a son of a bitch. I've heard him called the *evil king of Clark Street Cadillac.*"

Tex's face took on a look of concern as he sipped his beer.

"A couple of weeks ago," Tex said, "I heard a rumor that someone on my assembly line had been fired. A day later, I learned who'd gotten the axe and how it happened. The guy is colored—one of the only Negros working in a skilled line position at Clark. Solomon Smith—that's the guy's name. He is a good guy; been at Clark for a few years. I knew that Solomon supported his family back in Mississippi. Him and me, we sometimes talked about wishing we could go back home, but the money we make working on the line—it's just too good."

Tex looked off, took a deep breath, and exhaled. His thoughts appeared to be in another place.

When Tex turned his attention back to his housemates, he said, "Solomon was popular with the rank and file. He always worked hard; did his job well; and never bitched—even when our super gave him some awful crap—which happened a lot. A few days before he got fired, the super called Sol some shameful racist names. Word is that Sol complained to personnel about the super's racist comments. The lady in personnel must have passed that complaint right up to management. Silva—who runs the whole factory—is more racist than anybody else in the joint. Anyway, the next day, Solomon was given his pink slip."

Tex grimaced, then slowly shook his head from side to side.

"I told our steward that the union should grieve it. I asked him why that hadn't already happened. The union must have passed my complaints on to management because the next day, I got the pink slip. Management was flexing its power. It was letting all the workers know that Clark Street was not going to put up with any protests, sort of like saying, *Workers should shut the hell up and just do their work.*"

Tex looked off across the restaurant. There was pain in his voice as he said, "How could they do that to me? I'd been at Clark for almost seven years. And it's not right that the union didn't do anything to object. My steward just said, *Sorry Tex. That's just how it goes. You can't beat city hall.*"

Ossia and Rusty watched as Tex took a large forkful of his hot turkey sandwich, chewed it slowly, and then swallowed it.

After a long drink from his bottle of Bud, Tex said, "It's tough. I send most of each paycheck back home to my wife and kids."

Rusty responded, "Jeez, Tex. I didn't know about your family. That makes it even more horrible."

"Yup," Tex said. "Sure does. Ginger and I got married just before I enlisted in '41. I was fighting in the Philippines when Charlie was born. After I returned in '46, we had Frankie and Ellie. Anyway, the pressure is on. We got a mortgage on our place and Charlie is now in college. He was the first in my family to finish high school. We were so proud. And he will, sure as hell, be the first to get his college diploma."

Tex swallowed. "We never were able to get ahead financially. Finally, in '54, I decided I had to come up here and earn some real money. The pay's been good. But it's been lonely—all those years away from Ginger, away from the kids. I try to get back and visit once or twice a year. But yes, it gets awfully lonely."

Tex looked down. When he looked up, he said, "Sol told me that Ford and Chrysler are going to be doing some hiring before Christmas. He's trying to get on with one of them. I guess, I'll try to do the same. If I don't succeed, well, I'm screwed. I'll have to return to Texas with my tail between my legs."

"That's awful," said Rusty.

Ossia's face expressed concern. "Know you have family. John say. Maybe John learn from Jeannine. John know everything about everybody."

Tex took a long swig of beer and chuckled. "Figured John would know." He gave a smile and added, "But I don't wanna turn this into a pity party. Here's a change of subject, Ossia, Rusty told me Jeannine says your buddy, Edith the Ghost, is for real. Is that true?"

"Yes," responded Ossia with a laugh. "I always say you, *Edith exist*. No one believe except Jeannine. But it truth. Edith visit often. Sometimes, Edith my only friend."

"Can we meet Edith sometime?" Rusty asked.

"I ask her." Ossia added a soft smile before saying, "No promises. Edith do what Edith want. Nothing more." She laughed and added, "And nothing less."

Follow Through

Rusty was relieved that Ossia and Tex had forgiven him. But there was one more apology he had to give. He decided to get it over with. After he returned to his room and had thrown his jacket onto his bed, Rusty headed down to the second floor. He stood in front of John's door and listened to the steady tap, tap, tap of a typewriter. Then he knocked on John's door.

The typing stopped and John hollered, "Sorry, I don't buy Girl Scout cookies."

Rusty was feeling confident after reconciling with Ossia and Tex and in a celebratory mood after a few bottles of Budweiser. "It's Edith Beaulieu's favorite housemate," he said. "I'm here to haunt you."

"Please enter, Oh ghost of Edith's buddy."

John was sitting at his table, a small blue typewriter in front of him. Rusty looked around the room. Its layout was pretty similar to his own. He noticed a print of a Rembrandt self-portrait hanging on the wall above John's bed and an open paperback book, *The Short Stories of Leo Tolstoy*, laying print-side down on John's bed.

In unison, the two men said, "I owe you an apology...."

They laughed. Then Rusty said, "I get to go first."

"Go for it," said John.

For the third time that day, Rusty launched into his apology. "Jeannine stopped me this afternoon as I was returning from work. She asked me to come into her apartment."

"Sounds ominous," said John.

Rusty took a deep breath before delivering his apology. "Jeannine knew I had accused you, Ossia, and Tex of lying about discussing my past. She knew I hadn't believed Ossia's claim that a ghost had been eavesdropping on us after we got back from Grosse Point. After giving me a glass of wine—which totally surprised me because when she invited me in, I thought I was going to get kicked out of the building—Jeannine told me the ghost of Edith Beaulieu really does exist. I was on the spot. If I didn't accept Jeannine's saying *there is a ghost*, I would've had to accuse Jeannine of being a liar too."

John laughed and said, "I am sure that would have gone over like a lead balloon."

Rusty had a resigned look on his face. He closed his eyes for a second, then said, "Living in a building with a ghost? I still haven't wrapped my tiny brain around that one. But I'm working on it. Anyway, Jeannine made clear that you and Tex had kept your word not to discuss my burglary conviction with Ossia. Earlier this evening, I apologized to Ossia and Tex. Now, it's your turn. I'm here in front of you, eating more crow."

John laughed. "You accepted the existence of a ghost much more gracefully than I did several years ago when faced with the idea of a ghost of that old biddy. But I gotta be honest with you. I still have my doubts today."

John stood up and walked over to his bureau, opened the bottom drawer, and pulled out two cut crystal whiskey glasses and an almost full bottle of Wild Turkey.

John smiled and said, "Can I offer you a glass of excellent Kentucky bourbon—you know, something to wash down my apology?"

Rusty smiled and replied, "How could I turn down Wild Turkey with the aftertaste of eating crow still present?"

John poured some golden liquid into each of the cut crystal glasses. He handed one to Rusty; then held up the other and said, "Here's to humiliation."

Rusty grinned, raised his glass, and repeated, "To humiliation."

Rusty took a small taste. The bourbon was smooth. Its complex taste was sort of a mixture of nutty and vanilla. But there was also a little chocolate in there. He followed that taste up with a longer drink and ended up shaking his head at the kick delivered by the straight liquor.

John downed half his glass in one drink. Then he said, "OK. Here goes. My apology is more nuanced than yours. I am guilty of a succession of screw-ups here at the Green House over the last few years. The result? Now Ossia and Tex have stopped speaking with me. The only person in this place who'll still speak with me is Jeannine. And she told me I'd acted like a jerk—and added that I'd acted that way ever since I moved into the Green House. After she said that, I think she felt sorry for me. She added *All of us screw up sometimes.*"

John clinked glasses with Rusty and said, "So, back to the business of well-cooked humble pie, I apologize to you for aggressively butting into your life."

Rusty smiled, briefly tipped his head forward in acknowledgment of John's statement, and said, "Accepted. You are formally pardoned, John. The truth is that my having served time in prison makes me feel vulnerable—and I've felt that way too often in my life. Trying to start over while putting my conviction and prison time behind me has been more difficult than you could ever imagine."

"I'm sorry, Rusty," said John. "Seriously though, thank you. I appreciate being forgiven. Now, I've got to fix things with Tex and Ossia. I hope they'll be as receptive as you've been. They both are pissed at me. Tex accused me of destroying the whole sense of community in this house. I recognize he's probably right. If I hadn't been so set on butting into your business, none of this would have happened."

"You gotta stop pretending you're Sam Spade," said Rusty. Then he added, "However, I've got some good news for you. I just had dinner with Tex and Ossia. After I delivered my mea copas to them, they told me I had to speak with you and end the whole conflict."

John smiled and refilled each of their glasses with *Wild Turkey*. The two housemates drained their glasses a second time.

Once past the strong kick from downing a full glass of whiskey, Rusty gave a sly smile and said, "Given how guilty I got you feeling, I might as well push my luck. Ever since I met you, John, I've wondered about the fact that you know so much about everyone else's background—but no one around here knows anything about your life. What's your story, John? Tell me about your background. Given that you just drained that second glass of whiskey, I figure this might be the best time to ask."

John laughed and responded, "Smart call. I can't hold my liquor."

This time, it was Rusty who took the bottle of Wild Turkey and refilled their glasses.

"Finding out about other people," said John after downing half of the whiskey in his glass, "while not letting them learn anything about me—that's been my art form. Ordinarily, I'd give you a smooth brush-off on your question. But I don't think I'd get away with that today given what we've been through in the past month." He chuckled and completed his thought, "especially after this bourbon. No, tonight I'll probably give you a halfway honest response."

John sipped some whiskey, then continued. "Rusty. I can tell you this for certain. I was born at a young age."

Rusty started to protest that that response was bullshit. But John, still chuckling, raised his right hand, a signal to Rusty that he should hold off on any complaint.

"No, Rusty," he said. "I understand you will demand more of an answer than that. For once, I'm going to be open and honest. I was raised in Boston. My parents were both— how can I put it—from well-off families. Mother was one of those chicks who went to a bunch of debutante balls. Grandmother told me that Mother was regarded as quite the catch. Father went to Harvard as the proverbial overachieving student-athlete. After finishing law school, Father met Mother and swept her off of her feet. Once they were married, Father established himself as a highly successful capitalist. He navigated the Wall Street crash— actually made money off of it. By the time I was born in '35, my parents were pretty well set. I was their third child (I have two sisters). But *I* was the male heir—the prince waiting to become king."

John finished his glass and then went on with his story. "My parents had high expectations for their offspring. My sisters went to the right kind of girls-only colleges, found successful well-born husbands, and immediately started popping out grandbabies. However, what was most important for Father was that his only son, his heir, become a great success. You know, Father wanted to brag about me to his friends at the club. *Well, John did this and John won that and who knows, maybe someday John will be president of the whole goddamned country.* Things were looking pretty damn good after I got admitted to both Harvard and Princeton. The stage, as far as Father was concerned, was set for success. That's when Father's plan was shattered. I chose to escape from my parents' superficial blueprint for life, enrolled at Michigan State, and chose to study English literature. Father never forgave me for not getting a proper upper-class pedigree."

John poured each of them a fourth glass of the Wild Turkey before standing up and walking to the window. As he gazed out at a light snow that had begun to fall, he said, "Father cut me out of the family. He stopped speaking with me and removed me from their will. I worked my way through Michigan State waiting on tables. After graduating, I moved to Detroit, got this room, and went to work as a waiter. I work one shift a week at an expensive Dearborn steakhouse. I earn enough to cover my living costs. And the shiny red Chevy? I bought it a couple of years back with the remainder of the trust account my grandparents set up for me after I was born."

The whiskey had performed its magic and John's language had become slurred. "What do I do with my days? I sit in front of that fucking typewriter. I work on what I hope will someday be the next great American novel."

John sat down on the bed. Rusty was sitting on a chair across from him. For a few minutes, the two housemates sipped Wild Turkey, saying nothing.

Rusty broke the silence. "But we do have a problem neither of us created. That's the issue of Tex getting fired."

"Yeah," John said, "Jeannine told me about that. That's really the shits. What's Tex's plan?"

"He's trying to find work," said Rusty. "He says he'll have to move out of the Green House if he can't find another job. What's amazing is that the plant he works at is managed by the creep who owns the house we spied on."

John's simple reply was, "Yeah, Rusty. It's a small world."

*****

A week later on Saturday evening, Ossia, Rusty, John, and Tex sat around the table at Tony's Bar. It had taken five minutes for the four friends to devour their first extra-large pizza and Rusty was treating them to a second pizza which Charlie had just brought to the table along with a third pitcher of beer.

"Have good news," said Ossia. "You ask me speak Edith about you meet her. Edith say she ready meet you this week."

Three men gave double-takes at the same moment.

Rusty spoke up first. "Yeah, Ossia. I asked you if you'd talk to her. But I sort of thought the whole thing might never occur. Sounds like we are about to have a séance. Will we sit in a circle, maybe hold hands? Will we ask questions and hope to hear knocks under the table as a response?

Tex and John chortled.

"No Rusty," said Ossia with a disgusted look on her face. "You fool yourself believe you know way of world. This no joke. Sometimes, I see Edith. Sometimes, not see her; only hear. Edith always speak clear. I introduce you her. You have questions? You ask. She answer. I know she have questions. She ask you for something—maybe."

"What sort of thing will she ask for?" asked John.

"Edith speak for Edith. You have question. You ask her. We meet Wednesday evening, my room, seven o'clock? Everyone agree?"

The three men nodded.

"One thing more," Ossia said. "Edith ask this stay private. She say she trust Rusty for that. She trust Tex. But she have big concern John blab story. John, promise not blab?"

Rusty and Tex laughed.

John's face turned red and he rolled his eyes before saying, "You got it. Tell Edith my lips are sealed. That being said, if we only hear her voice, how will we know it's not Jeannine—who also has a French accent—pretending to be a ghost as she speaks from a closet or through a speaker from another room?"

Ossia gave a sly smile. "Maybe you not believe? That your problem, John. Not mine. Rusty ask me set up. Now, set up."

The discussion over, the four friends turned their attention to pizza and beer.

A few minutes later, Tex said, "I have some really good news."

"Let's have it," said John. "Try to make it as interesting as Ossia's—if that's possible."

Tex smiled and said, "I can't pull that off, John. But my news is good—at least for me. Yesterday, I got called in for an orientation interview at Dodge Hamtramck. I start working the day shift there in December. That means I won't have to move from the Green House!"

Ossia, said, "*Nostrovia*—health and happiness."

The housemates lifted their glasses and the toast was repeated by all.

Tex added, "There were about fifteen of us at the interview. One of them was Solomon Smith, the colored guy I told you about who got fired at Clark Street. Anyway, Sol also got hired. He was in the same orientation group as me. After the interview, we went out for a beer to celebrate."

Tex's tone changed. "Solomon told me he already had given notice at his place and someone had put down a rent deposit on it. So, Sol has to move. He asked if I knew of any places for rent. I told him there might be a vacant room at the Green House. He was interested. When I told

Jeannine about it, she didn't respond too warmly. She told me she had never had a colored person as a tenant. Then she paused, seemed to think about it for a moment, and said, *Well, things seem to be changing. I guess I need to be open to change. Have Solomon stop by. If I like him, I'll consider renting a room to him."*

After saying that, Tex picked up his guitar and made his way up to the bar's small stage where he began his set.

As he introduced his first song, Tex smiled and said, "I'm dedicating this first one," he said, "to a few of my friends."

Then Tex performed Elvis's classic *Heartbreak Hotel.*

A Séance—of Sorts

After arriving at Ossia's room a few minutes late that Wednesday evening, Rusty saw that John and Tex were already seated on the settee. After opening the door for him, Ossia returned to her chair and Rusty sat on a stool next to the settee.

A moment later, a voice with a melodic French accent came from across the room. "*Bienvenue.* Many thanks to each of you for honoring my invitation."

The housemates turned. At first, they saw no one. John looked like he was about to make a wisecrack about Edith being invisible when the soft, semi-transparent features of a dark-eyed older woman gradually materialized in front of them. Edith was dressed in a white-lace, long-sleeved blouse with a long navy-blue skirt. Her grey hair was pinned above her head, held in place by a dramatic pearl hair clip.

As the apparition glided toward them from across the room, Edith continued to speak. "I chose to be visible this evening after Ossia warned me that John, your house cynic, would not be convinced he was speaking with a spirit if he could not see her. Well, John, here I am."

The three men sat in wide-eyed silence.

Ossia said, "Edith and I talk how meeting go. She say you ask questions."

Rusty wasn't surprised that John responded to that invitation without hesitation. "Yes, Edith. I do have a question for you. How do we know you are real and not just some sort of fancy illusion?"

The ghost of Edith gave a soft laugh before saying, "John, I choose to ignore your question because I realize you often do not think before you speak. *Ce soir*, you will have to decide whether I exist—or whether you just dream of me. Or maybe I have been conjured up by the skillful magician, Madam Ossia who has somehow fooled your simple mind."

The gray-haired ghost smiled before adding, "Deciding whether I exist—or not—this is your problem, John, not mine."

John seemed a little humbled by Edith's words and gave no smart, snarky comeback to her statement. Tex and Rusty, despite being fully amazed by her appearance, couldn't hold back their laughter.

Edith continued. "Before I say why I wanted to meet with the four of you today, Tex, Rusty—do either of you have a question?"

Tex said, "Maybe later, Edith. This is sort of new territory for me. But pleased to meet you."

"Likewise," said Edith. "And Tex, I appreciate how you always behave like a gentleman."

Rusty said, "I have no questions either. But thank you, Edith, for meeting with us."

"It is my pleasure," said Edith. "Now, my request. About a month ago, John and Rusty visited the beautiful home in which I once lived, a place I call the *White House*. John mused on how he might gain entry. It is that possible action which I wish to explore with you this evening."

Ossia had placed a second stool near the housemates. Edith sat down on it and then continued to speak. "After my husband took his life in the panicked stock market of 1929, a part-owner of the bank from which Edwin had borrowed a small amount manipulated the laws of this country to steal my home. This man's name was Silva. He paid the small debt that Edwin owed to the bank; then took possession of the White House including all of its elegant furnishings and my precious paintings. In listening to John, I learned that another Silva, the original thief's child, now owns my cherished home. And based upon what Tex said, I know this younger Silva is just as much a pig as his lecherous father."

Edith's ghost stood up and walked across Ossia's room. She stopped facing the window and gazed outside at a delicate snowfall. The three male housemates watched her in stunned silence.

After a few quiet moments, Edith turned to the housemates and said, "For the twelve years since I passed, I have been a prisoner in the Green House—unable to travel anywhere else. However last month, on that glorious Wednesday, I was transported to another place for the first time since my death. Yes. I was returned to my wonderful White House."

The ghost of Edith returned to the stool across from the others and said, "I was with John and Rusty when they approached the White House. *C'etait extroardinaire!* After more than a decade, I had been once again transported to the home I love. I watched as the two of you walked from that shiny red automobile to the door. I listened with joy to the doorbell's lovely chimes. When John passed through the gate into the garden, I was amused and impressed how he bought the love of that obnoxious dog with a simple cookie."

Rusty realized that neither he nor John had told anyone about John's trick with the dog biscuit. This was an unintended confirmation that Edith's appearance wasn't a gimmick—that was unless John was in on an elaborate prank. But that was nonsense. Rusty was certain that Edith was real.

The housemates waited in awe to hear what Edith would say next.

"I saw you," she said, "as you gazed through the backyard picture window into my living room. I observed with pride your response to my elegant furniture—although John, you were terribly disrespectful in your comments about my precious paintings."

John's face turned crimson. He looked down at the oak floor and muttered a quiet, "Sorry, Edith."

Edith ignored John's insipid apology as she continued. "How was I able to travel to the White House with John and Rusty? *Je ne sais pas.* My heart was once again full to be at my home—to be inside my home. Because while John and Rusty gazed into the living and dining rooms through their windows, I was able to easily pass through the walls into the rooms and halls of my wonderful *Blanc Chateau.* I found joy in seeing my watercolors, pastels, and oil paintings. Those art pieces are the diary of my life."

Edith was silent for a couple of moments before saying, "My art studio was the sunroom on the south side of the home. Its east window looks out upon Lake St. Clair. Working in that studio during the twenty years I lived in that house, I painted many happy visions. My most treasured achievement was created in that studio during the winter of 1924-1925. It was a tryptic—three paintings that told the story of a single enchanted dream, a reverie that reflected my childhood in France. The paintings told the story of my papa, mama, and me, a mélange of joy and sadness. Before telling you why I speak about those special works now, it would give me great pleasure to be able to describe the three compositions."

Edith gazed across the room as if she was seeing the works she was about to describe. "Looking at the three oil paintings from left to right, the first one showed Papa at work at his easel. He was painting a marvelous orchard of red, yellow, and pink apples growing on maroon trees. And there, standing among the trees, were Papa, Mama, and me surrounded by rainbows and bluebirds against a blue sky with pillowy clouds."

Edith interrupted the description of the tryptic with a deep, satisfied sigh. Then she gave a smile and continued. "The center painting of the tryptic showed Mama at her kitchen table making an apple tart in our toasty Paris kitchen. Papa and I were sitting on stools next to her, watching her slice those multi-colored apples. Through the painting's kitchen window, you can see the orchard, the bluebirds, and the rainbows. And there, off on a hill in the orchard, you see once again Mama, Papa, and me dancing together in a small circle."

Edith smiled, took another deep breath, and exhaled. A moment later, her face took on a serious look as she said, "In the third painting, shimmering light is provided by a large yellow moon on a dark blue night full of sparkling stars. In the center of this composition, Papa and Mama stand by a small pond, holding one another's hand. They weep as they gaze into the pond. They see me—their daughter—smiling up at them from down in the pond. I am holding an apple tart in one hand and several of Papa's colorful paintbrushes in the other."

Edith took a deep breath, brushed away a tear, and said, "My agent—the man who sold my paintings—when he saw the tryptic, he said, *I have a buyer who will pay thousands for this tryptic, Edith.* I told him, *Non, absolutement non. I will not sell.* After that, Edwin—my husband—said, *You should sell them, Edith. That's a lot of money.*"

The ghost of Edith closed her eyes and shook her head slowly from side to side while saying, "But I could not sell those paintings. They were like my children. I feared that my agent would pressure Edwin and that Edwin, in turn, would pressure me. So, early one morning, before Edwin awoke, I sneaked out of our bedroom and carefully wrapped those three lovely paintings in tarps. I took them up to the attic, covered them with insulation, and bid them *au revoir.*"

Edith whose back had been to her listeners turned toward the four housemates and said slowly, "The next day, Edwin saw the three paintings were gone, disappeared from their easels. He asked me, *Where are your lovely paintings, dearest? I* said to him, *They are gone, Edwin. I do not know where.* Edwin knew, of course, that I had taken the tryptic. But he did not know where the three paintings had been hidden."

The housemates watched as tears rolled down the ghost's cheeks. They waited, continuing to give total attention to this visitor from the past, totally attentive to what she might say next.

"Time passed," Edith continued in a soft voice. "I forgot my lovely paintings. This October, I was able, somehow, to arrive—with John and Rusty—at my wonderful White House. Suddenly, I was flooded with memories of those three dear creations. Those paintings are my connection to my Mama and Papa—and yes, *peut etre* to my own soul. My dear guests, I want to see these paintings again. I don't know if the graces of the universe will allow me to accompany you to my dear White House a second time. But whether I am able to accompany you or not, retrieving those paintings from their hidden safe spot is my greatest wish."

Edith sat down on the stool and gazed across the room.

A moment later, she shook her head as if coming out of a daze and said, "It doesn't make a difference whether I am with you—or not. If you go to the White House, if you enter the home and climb into the attic, if you find my dear creations wrapped in those tarps, still covered with insulation, under the roof's west eve, please bring them here—to me—to my Green House. This is what I ask of you."

After saying this, Edith Beaulieu slowly stood up, walked across the room and, as if to remind them that they had been listening to a spirit, the gray-haired ghost disappeared through the wall.

Next Steps

The four housemates sat together drinking lotus blossom tea out of Ossia's colorful mugs. For a quarter of an hour after Edith had disappeared, not a word was spoken.

Finally, John broke the ice when he uttered, "Wow."

Tex followed that up with, "I'll see your *wow*, John, and raise it a *holy shit*."

Ossia, obviously trying to hide her smile, softly said, "I say many times, *Edith exist*. No. You laugh. You think Ossia silly. Ossia look silly now?"

Rusty said nothing. Seeing the ghost had been shocking. But he was also facing a different dilemma. A ghost had asked him to break into a home. This issue, which had separated the four housemates a month before, had turned out to be the basis of why they came together that evening. Rusty had been adamant that he would not do anything that could result in his returning to a life behind bars. Now, whether he liked it or not, he was being pressured to reconsider such a plan. What should he do?

Tex brought Rusty's conundrum to the fore. "Are we all so quiet because we are afraid to say the two words, *Grosse Point*?"

John rolled his eyes. "I know better than to get into that," he said. "I already messed up with all of you on that subject already."

Ossia said, "I not surprised Edith request. She tell me before. Understand this difficult you, Rusty."

Everyone looked at Rusty.

"Okay," he said. "You are all waiting for me to tell you what I think. I can't ask you, *What did I do to be put into such an uncomfortable position?* You guys know the answer to that question already."

The others continued to watch Rusty.

After a minute of silence, Rusty said, "In answer to your obvious question, I am totally confused about what to do. Of course, we could drive out there. Ossia could stay in the car—parked a few doors down—watching the place. She could honk the horn if someone showed up. Tex, John, and I could go around the side of the house."

With the others watching him closely, Rusty stopped speaking. He was trying to visualize how he would approach the break-in.

Ossia interrupted his reverie by saying, "If I outside, how I see paintings?"

Ossia answered her own question a moment later. "I know. You take my Kodak Brownie camera. Use new roll color film. Photograph Edith paintings for me."

"You got it, Ossia." chimed in John. "That would do the trick."

John, looking at Rusty, said, "But how do we get into the house?"

Rusty's housemates waited.

"OK. I know how to disarm that alarm," said Rusty. "It's a piece of cake. I noticed there is a window near the alarm that would be a snap to jimmy open."

Rusty stopped speaking. The others waited.

Rusty sighed and said, "If I choose to participate in this in any way, it won't make a lick of difference whether I go into the home or stay outside. The cops will arrest me in a heartbeat and the DA will name me the mastermind. There is no point in my going halfway. I'm either in this all the way or I'm not participating at all."

Rusty's housemates were silent.

After what seemed like a long time, Rusty said, "I need to think this through. Can we get together tomorrow evening?"

The housemates agreed to meet at seven the following evening. The three men bid Ossia *sweet dreams* and headed up to their rooms.

*****

During the following workday, things were intense at the hospital. A severe car accident in downtown Detroit resulted in half a dozen emergency room patients needing urgent care at the same time. Rusty and his coworkers rushed between the emergency room, the intensive care unit, and various surgery rooms throughout the entire shift. There wasn't a moment for Rusty to consider whether he should participate in a suburban house break-in.

A light snow was falling as Rusty headed home at the end of his shift. As he walked, Rusty considered his options. He decided there were only two alternatives. Tell the others he wasn't participating or tell them he was in and go for it. If he participated, he would be committing a serious felony—breaking, entering and he would certainly be accused of attempted robbery. Given his prior conviction, there could be no doubt he would be named the crime's ringleader. He would probably end up in a state prison for at least a decade.

The circumstances were unusual. A ghost—a being whose life had ended—had prevailed upon him to act. Should the fact that a supernatural being was pressuring him be a factor in his decision? How would he feel afterward if he chose to ignore that spirit's single request? On the other hand, would going to jail seem any less harsh if it had been driven by gallantry on behalf of a ghost?

When he arrived at the rooming house, he was relieved that none of his housemates saw him as he walked up to his room. He lay down on his bed while he tried to figure out what he should say to his housemates when he met with them a few hours later.

Rusty was tired. Within minutes, he had fallen asleep. It was then that he had a dream about his mother.

***

Rusty's mother had been dead for almost a decade, now. Rusty was certain she would have been deeply ashamed if she had known he had committed burglaries and had served time in prison. He had never shared with anyone that not living up to his mother's expectations had been a greater emotional burden for him than serving eighteen months in a state prison.

In Rusty's dream, he woke up and saw his mother standing at the side of his bed.

"Ma!" he said. "Is that you?"

"Yes, It's me, Sonny. And before you say anything, sweetheart, I know about your crimes in Ann Arbor. Even though I'm not proud of you for stealing, you were young and your world had just fallen apart. You were also pretty stupid to do what you did, Sonny. But you made your bad choices and I know you've paid a steep price."

In the dream, Rusty sat up in his bed. The circumstance seemed even more bizarre after he saw that Edith Beaulieu was standing in a corner of his room watching his mother as she spoke.

"I only have a little time," his mother said. "I'm not here to talk about your past. I am here because Edith has requested that I speak with you. Edith wants you to help get her paintings out of that big old house. Sonny, I want you to cooperate with her and with your housemates. You did bad stuff with what you learned from Mr. Erickson about alarms. Now, you have a chance to use that knowledge for a good purpose."

"Ma. Will I ever see you again? Where—how—what is happening? Is this a dream?"

"Sonny, you remember that time you woke up in the middle of the night when there was all of that lightning and thunder? I think you were about six. I came into your room and saw you'd wet the bed. You were crying. I got you out of bed and had you put on clean jammies. After I changed the bedding, you got back into bed. But you were still scared. Do you remember what I did?"

"Yes, I do, Ma."

"Okay. Roll over and go back to sleep."

And in his dream, Rusty's mother rubbed his back until he'd fallen asleep.

When Rusty woke up, he was confused. He was still fully clothed and it wasn't morning. Then he remembered he had taken a nap after work.

Rusty realized he was hungry. He climbed out of bed, opened a can of chili, put it in the pan, and started heating it. Suddenly, he remembered his unusual dream. Yes. In the dream, his mother had spoken to him. She had been there with Edith Beaulieu. For a moment, Rusty wondered if maybe he had actually been visited by his mother's spirit. Maybe she had come to him at the request of the ghost of the French lady who had owned the Green House.

"Nah," he thought to himself. "That's too far-fetched."

He paused for a moment, then extended that thought, "But a ghost in the house is already pretty weird. Strange occurrences seem to be occurring in my life."

Rusty closed out his contemplation by saying to himself, "Looks like my house break-in days aren't over."

The chili was ready. He grabbed a spoon and ate his dinner out of the pan.

Meetings and Planning

After Rusty had eaten, he went to Ossia's room to continue their previous night's discussion. His housemates had already arrived. There was a plate of butter cookies, four mugs, and a pot of Constant Comment Tea on Ossia's small table.

After pleasantries were exchanged, Rusty started it off. "Did we really meet the old lady last night or did I just dream it? I'm hoping it was the latter."

Tex and John laughed. Ossia gave a look of disdain.

Tex said, "I struggled with that question all day. Either this is a continuation of *my* dream or we met a ghost last night."

John (who had already eaten two butter cookies) displayed a business-like focus. "Let's dig into this, guys—and of course, you too, Ossia. I went out to Grosse Point today and checked out our target one more time—just to be thorough. I'm certain we can do this. The only question is whether Rusty is on board. Because if he's not, let's drink our tea, eat our cookies, and go get some sleep."

Three sets of eyes turned to Rusty. He looked at the ceiling for a minute. This was his last chance to think through his options.

"OK," said Rusty. "Here's my answer. I'm in. Let's start planning."

The other three waited for Rusty to say more.

"The alarm's not an issue," Rusty said. "I could disable it in my sleep. And getting into the house won't be difficult. That window I mentioned yesterday looks like it's been opened and closed a lot. That sort of internal clasp is a piece of cake to unlatch. The as yet unanswered questions are *Who goes in?* and *When?*"

Tex responded. "I identified the *when*—a time when Silva will probably be out of town. This morning, while I was waiting at the barbershop to get my haircut, I leafed through an auto industry magazine. I saw that there's an auto exec convention in Chicago in mid-December. General Motor's CEO will give a big speech at the convention banquet on Saturday, December 15. The theme of his speech is that this year is the sixtieth anniversary of Cadillac. Since Silva is the general manager of the main Cadillac assembly plant, I gotta believe he's gonna be there. We could do it that Saturday."

The three other housemates nodded their concurrence.

"Sounds good," said John. "Ok, time for my update. When I did a reconnaissance of Grosse Point this morning, I noticed a small playground up the block and across the street from the house. When we break in—I guess that's going to be on the 15th now—I'll park in front of the playground. I got a brainstorm for how we can stay in touch with Ossia in the car while the rest of us are in the house. Radio Shack sells a set of walkie-talkies for $19.95. They can transmit and receive conversations for up to a quarter of a mile. Using them, Ossia can let us know if anyone approaches the house."

Ossia laughed and said, "I lookout." She took a sip of tea, gave a thoughtful expression and added, "Speak with Edith later. Make sure her approve."

John said, "I have no doubt Edith is listening right now."

Ossia smiled.

Tex had a worried look. "This all sounds fine to me. But I got a question. If John, Rusty, and I are up in the attic and Ossia calls to let us know Silva has returned home, what do we do?"

There was silence in the room until John said, "Hell, Tex. You worry too damn much. Relax. The sky ain't gonna fall."

*****

On Saturday, December 1, Solomon Smith moved into the Green House. The following Monday, Solomon and Tex began work at Dodge Hamtramck. That evening, Tex treated Ossia, Rusty, and John to dinner at the Woodward Avenue Diner to celebrate his new job.

After the housemates sat down in their booth and ordered their dinners, John asked, "How'd it go, Tex?"

Tex, who had just taken a sip of beer, put down his bottle of Budweiser and said, "Everything went well. Bus connections to the plant were perfect. Sol and I caught the 5:55 bus on Woodward, transferred at Holbrook, and were at the plant by 6:45. The two of us along with twenty-five other new workers spent the morning at an orientation. We learned plant safety rules and filled out personnel forms. After lunch, we were taken out to our line stations. That was weird. Hamtramck is the biggest, noisiest manufacturing facility you can imagine! It took them fifteen minutes to walk me to my station!"

Tex stopped speaking as the waitress delivered cheeseburgers and fries to the men and a cobb salad to Ossia.

Before digging into his burger, Tex said. "My foreman showed me my routine. Every fifty seconds, another halfway-built Dodge rolls down the line. When the car is right in front of me, I slide its transmission into position on its chassis. Then secure it into that position with a half dozen bolts. The car continues to roll along but I turn around and there is another automobile heading toward me, ready for me to repeat my magic."

Rusty, John, and Ossia had never worked in an automobile factory and paid close attention to Tex's description. Once he finished describing Hamtramck's assembly line experience, everyone's attention turned to their food.

After they'd finished their dinners, Ossia said, "No one ask what help I bring."

John rolled his eyes but Tex said, "I'm sorry Ossia. That's typical of guys. Men know it all and ignore what women might offer. Explain to us what you mean."

Ossia held back a smile as she removed a folded piece of paper from her purse.

"When Edith describe rooms inside White House," she said, "I make her talk slow; draw map of White House."

Ossia unfolded the drawing. It was a floor plan for both floors of the White House. On the first floor, the home's main entry was across from a two-flight staircase to the second floor. A large living room was on the entry's left. Further on, there was a sunroom. To the right of the entry was a hallway that led past a study and a half-bath ending up at the kitchen. At the back of the home, between the kitchen and the living room, was a dining room.

The floor plan for the second floor showed a two-flight staircase emerging onto a small hallway at the front of the home. Above the living room was a large master bedroom and attached bath. The other side of the floor had a front and back bedroom separated by a bathroom. That back bedroom had a closet with a stairway inside. It led to the attic. Ossia's map had an *X* marked near the top of the attic's steps.

"X mark," said Ossia, "show where Edith hide paintings under insulation. She say easy find paintings."

Rusty said, "Wow! This is really useful, Ossia. Way to go!"

Ossia smiled and made a small *so-there* face at John.

Tex had a puzzled look on his face. "Sorry to sidetrack us," he said, "but I been wondering about something for a while now. I think we can do this and I think we'll probably succeed—I mean we'll get Edith Beaulieu's paintings. That's all fine and dandy. Let's assume we pull it off and get the three paintings. What are we going to do with them?"

There was a moment's silence at the table before Ossia said, "I ask Edith."

*****

A few days later, John rapped on Rusty's door. After Rusty invited him in, John said, "I bought the walkie-talkies. I think we need to rehearse using them."

"John, you're an idiot," was Rusty's quick retort. "You are turning something simple into something complex. That's not an advantage. That's a says disadvantage."

Despite being disgusted with John's approach, Rusty agreed to get together with the others in John's room for a rehearsal on the following Tuesday evening—just four days before they planned to go into Silva's home.

Solomon's Story

Solomon Smith was the first person to move into the Green House since Rusty had taken his room one year before. Rusty remembered how he had felt like such an outsider before meeting Tex. With that in mind, he decided to make an effort to have Solomon feel more welcome than he had when he was the newest tenant. On Saturday morning, December 8th, Rusty went to Solomon Smith's room to introduce himself.

As Rusty was about to knock on Solomon's door, he recognized the soft bluesy sound of a mouth organ coming from Sol's room. The mouth organ is an inexpensive musical instrument that can produce a whole range of emotions. It is not expensive to acquire—an inmate can easily afford it. Rusty had had a few friends at the state prison who were quite skilled in its use and he had often enjoyed listening to their music while he was in the joint.

Rusty stood in front of Solomon's door and listened to the sound of a blues harp for a moment before knocking.

The medium-height, dark-skinned man who opened the door asked, "Can I help you, buddy?"

"My name's Rusty. I live on the third floor. I was the last new tenant in the Green House. A few days after I moved in, Tex went out of his way to make me feel welcome. I wanted to do the same for you."

Solomon appeared to relax as he said, "Tex is a pretty good dude. We both went through hell at Clark Street. I appreciated him having my back there as well as his telling me about the vacancy here."

Rusty replied, "And your telling Tex about the opening at Hamtramck was a lifesaver as far as he is concerned."

Solomon chuckled and replied, "Yeah. Tex's been pretty clear that getting on at Hamtramck was a good thing."

"Have any other Green House residents welcomed you since you moved in?" asked Rusty.

Solomon chuckled again before saying, "I'm not sure how to respond to that, Rusty. You're the first person here to speak a word to me—other than Tex, of course. Oh, and Jeannine, as well—you know, when she rented me the room."

"I hope you end up feeling good about living here," said Rusty. "I don't know everyone at the Green House. But each person I've met has been nice."

Solomon smiled and said, "That's great. I look forward to seeing them."

There was an uncomfortable silence in the room. Rusty wondered if maybe he ought to leave. Then he had an idea.

"On Saturday evenings," he said, "a few of us sometimes go out and listen to Tex perform at Tony's Bar. Tex sings and accompanies himself on the Dobro. We're heading there this evening at seven. Why don't you join us?"

"Tex mentioned his Saturday gigs," said Solomon. "Told me that tonight, you might be the only other person from this rooming house to go. I told him I'd think about it. Sounds like Tony's is a good old boy's bar. I'm wondering how welcome someone with my tone of skin color would be. You know, I've never really qualified as a good ole boy. Anyway, thanks for the invite. I'll think about it. If I decide to join you, I'll see you in front of the Green House at seven."

"I think the folks there would be fine, Solomon—and that you'd enjoy it. I hope you come."

"Thanks, Rusty. By the way, my friends call me Sol. I'd like it if you did the same."

"Thanks, Sol. Hope to see you later."
*****

That evening, as Rusty headed out of the Green House, he saw Tex and Solomon waiting on the sidewalk in front of the building.

"I thought about it and decided I couldn't pass up an evening with free pizza, beer, and white folks," said Solomon Smith.

"I'm relieved that you're coming," responded Rusty. "I was afraid I was going to have to spend the evening listening to Tex tell me how big the State of Texas is."

Tex jumped in with, "What's wrong with talking about Texas? It's the biggest damn state in the union."

Rusty didn't bother to correct Tex by mentioning Alaska had become a state. They had had that mock argument too many times before. The three men laughed and continued to joke as they headed up the street to Tony's Bar.

When they entered Tony's a short while later, Charlie the bartender raised his eyebrows. Conversations across the bar stopped as Tony's regulars turned to look at the three housemates heading over to Tex's regular table.

As they sat down, Tex said in a subdued voice, "We must be awfully good-looking because everybody's watching us."

"I noticed," said Solomon. "I think they kind of think that I'm the really handsome one."

Charlie brought a pitcher of beer and three glasses. After he put the pitcher on the table, he paused for a moment, then asked, "Regular pizza—extra-large with the works?"

"You got it," said Tex.

Others in the bar returned to their conversations, paying little attention to the trio. For the next fifteen minutes, Rusty listened to Tex and Solomon speak about the people they worked with throughout their years at the Clark Assembly Plant. However, once Charlie put the pizza on the table, their attention turned to enjoying dinner.

After they'd finished the pizza and had consumed a second pitcher of beer, Tex said, "Time to earn my keep."

He opened his guitar case, lifted up the Dobro, and walked up to the small stage. After taking a moment to tune his slide guitar, Tex started playing a series of country and western hits. His audience applauded the loudest for his renditions of Hank Williams' *Your Cheating Heart*, Marty Robbins' *El Paso*, and Roy Rogers' *Tumblin Tumbleweeds*.

In between sets, the threesome drank another pitcher and joked about the differences between country music tastes in Mississippi, Texas, and Michigan.

Later on, for his second set of the evening, Tex led off with an exaggerated imitation of Johnny Cash's deep voice while singing *I Walk the Line*. The bar was packed and the patrons all turned their chairs toward the stage and started clapping with the beat of the music as Tex sang.

I keep a close watch on this heart of mine
I keep my eyes wide open all the time
I keep the ends out for the tie that binds
Because you're mine, I walk the line

After finishing the song, Tex said in his casual Texas drawl, "You know, I generally perform solo. But tonight, I'm making an exception to that rule. In this second set, I'm gonna do a few instrumentals with a pal of mine. A couple of evenings ago, I was in my room, playing the Dobro, when a buddy of mine stopped by. He listens for a while, then he whipped out his mouth organ and started playing along with me. I moved into a series of pieces I don't ordinarily play here at Tony's—favorites you all know from the fifties. My buddy kept up with me. And you know? Damned if it didn't sound pretty nice. So, to make a long story short, my buddy, Solomon Smith is here tonight and I want to invite him up and we can share with you a few of those numbers. Solomon—would you head on up here and bring your harp?"

Rusty looked at Solomon whose expression revealed he had been caught totally off guard. There was quiet in the bar as the black man stood up, reached into his pants pocket, pulled out his small harmonica, and headed up to the stage.

The room was quiet as Tex hit the opening strains of Patti Page's *The Tennessee Walz*. At the chorus, Solomon joined in. The audience seemed to relax as they listened to the two musicians work together on the sentimental ballad. Polite applause followed the song. Tex moved from that right into Hank Williams' *Hey Good Lookin*. Then Tex changed the fare as he moved into Fats Domino's *Blueberry Hill*. Solomon seemed to get into it adding a few riffs. That inspired Tex to respond in kind. As they performed, the audience's applause increased after each succeeding classic hit. Solomon and Tex were working together as if they'd been performing duets for years. The audience began to whoop and holler as the duo got into each additional song.

Among the hits, they played were Elvis's *Love Me Tender*, Ray Charles' *I Got a Woman,* and The Platters' *Only You.*

When Tex stated in his soft manner, "That's all folks," the now-rowdy crowd started chanting, "One more song. One more song."

Tex looked at Solomon and said *"Jambalaya."* Solomon nodded and Tex started playing the Hank Williams classic. As they performed, the two artists watched one another and took turns improvising riffs off of that song of celebration. The crowd went nuts.

Sol and Tex sang the song's final chorus together.

Jambalaya and a crawfish pie and fillet gumbo
'Cause tonight I'm gonna see my ma cher amio
Pick guitar, fill fruit jar and be gay-o
Son of a gun we'll have big fun on the bayou.

As Tex and Solomon returned to their seats, Rusty was standing and applauding along with everyone else in the bar.

A few minutes later, Tex packed up his guitar and the three housemates headed out of Tony's. As they passed the bar, Charlie nodded his approval and said, "Nice work Tex. And Solomon—you're welcome here anytime you like. Just bring that mouth organ. That was sweet."

*****

A light snow was falling on the three housemates as they walked along a quiet Warren Avenue on their way home from Tony's.

Rusty broke the silence. "That was weird. I couldn't believe how quiet the place got when we walked in—and it did it again when Sol went up to perform. I've never experienced anything like that. Nice job, both of you. Way to keep cool while putting out some really fine sounds in an uncomfortable environment."

Tex said, "Sorry to catch you off guard, Sol. I knew you had your harp with you. I saw you fiddling with it while we waited for the pizza. I figured it would be cool for us to perform a few duets. The crowd got into it. But I apologize for putting you on the spot."

"Yeah, they did get into it—eventually," Solomon agreed with a chuckle. "But saying you *put me on the spot, Tex?* That may be a bit of an understatement. When I walked up there to join you, I wasn't feeling too comfortable. I think a few of our fans might have wanted to throw me out of the joint."

"Sorry," said Tex.

"Anyway," Sol said with a sigh, "I'm glad it turned out the way it did. And I like the way you work that Dobro, Tex. Some evening, when you're feeling adventurous, I'm gonna drag you along to one of my hangouts. I've jammed in a lot of joints in this city; But never before a white crowd. There's some really fine music coming out of Motown," said Solomon, "and most of it isn't performed by a white dude wearing a cowboy hat."

They walked for a while in silence.

"How's everything else going?" asked Tex.

"I'll put it out there straight," said Solomon. "I'm the outsider in this here Green House. To be fair, no one has said or done anything offensive. Still, I'm not completely enjoying the respectful silent treatment. I'm the building's invisible man. I guess I can live with that while I'm hanging low and figuring out what's next in my life."

"I appreciate that," said Rusty, "as well as the other personal things you shared earlier today. "When I first got into Marquette Prison, I felt awfully alone. The Negro half of the population ignored me and the white guys—well, they were a pretty tough and unfriendly crew. After a few days, I decided I was a whole lot better off with the folks of color. I ended up making some really special friends during my time there. But I also saw a hell of a lot of racism."

Solomon lit a Kool Menthol Cigarette before saying, "For me, Detroit's been a process of getting schooled in one new area after another. I came up here from Mississippi to help out my family. Unlike Tex, I wasn't sending paychecks home to a wife and kids. I was sending 'em for my mom, granddad, brothers, and sisters. Before I came up here, my family was barely getting by. I was the oldest kid and had had some sort of job since I was ten. But after high school, I knew I needed to help out more. That's why I came up here. Then I got on at Clark and shared a place with my uncle. After he moved back to Mississippi, I stayed. I've been alone a lot over the past few years. But my family, down there in Mississippi? They haven't been hungry."

"I can echo what you're saying about the money," chimed in Tex. "No way could I earn this kind of dough down South that I get here."

The three housemates walked in silence in the light snow.

After a few blocks, Solomon said, "Rusty, you mentioned racism. A lot of folks feel I ought to be relieved to be away from Mississippi. But the way folks up here do racism, it ain't so good either. White folks up here, they just don't mix with colored folks. Case in point, if it weren't for

Tex, I'd never have known about, or gotten a room in, the Green House."

The snow stopped and the street took on a peaceful air as the three housemates made their way home.

Sol continued, "Up here when I get stopped on the street by a cop and asked what I'm doing, where I was, or where I'm going, I better call the man in blue *sir*. I sure as hell shouldn't look him in the eye while I deliver a quick, simple answer to any question he poses. Too many brothers have ended up in the emergency room after a run-in with Detroit's finest. In Motown, police don't need a reason. All they gotta do is decide they don't like your attitude. It's a different flavor of hate from what I experienced back home—but it's just as vicious."

The three housemates didn't speak during the rest of their walk to the rooming house. When the men got to the second floor, Solomon turned down the hall to go to his room. Rusty said, "Thanks, Sol. Thanks for being straight with us. I'm glad you moved in."

*****

The next morning, the sun was shining brightly as Rusty went on his weekly trek to the Piggly Wiggly for the coming week's food provisions. As he exited the Green House, Sol was a couple of hundred yards ahead of him, going in the same direction.

"Heh, Sol," Rusty shouted. "Grocery store run?"

Sol turned, gave a wave, and responded, "A man's gotta eat."

Solomon Smith waited for Rusty to catch up and the two walked together.

After they had exchanged a few pleasantries about the weather, Rusty said, "Except for yesterday, I haven't seen you around a whole lot. You sure keep a low profile."

"I've been here, Rusty. Like I said, I'm the Green House's invisible man."

After they finished shopping, the two men carried their bags of groceries back to the Green House.

While they walked, Sol described the Hamtramck auto factory. "It's big. Working there, you feel like you are part of a machine, the screeching, the pounding noise, the endless assembly lines, and the constant motion. It's crazy. But the money's good."

Solomon chuckled, then asked, "Did you ever see Charlie Chaplin's film *Modern Times*? That movie lays it out pretty good."

Rusty said he had seen it. The two men laughed about the scene where Chaplin had bananas stuffed in his face by a machine during a mechanized lunch break.

As they approached the Green House, Solomon asked Rusty, "Wanna stop by for a beer?"

"A beer sounds really good," responded Rusty. "I'll put away my groceries. Then I'll be down."

*****

Fifteen minutes later, Sol welcomed Rusty into his room, handed him a bottle of Hamm's Beer, and invited him to sit down next to his small table upon which sat a bowl of pretzels. Rusty sat down, sipped his beer, and took a pretzel. He looked around Sol's room. The biggest difference from Rusty's room was that Solomon had a small bookcase under his windowsill. It held a couple of dozen books. Rusty looked at their titles. He wasn't familiar with any of them. But one book caught his attention. It was titled *The Invisible Man.*

"Earlier," Rusty said, "you called yourself *the Green House's invisible man*. I see a book with that title on your bookcase. Any connection?"

"Sure is," responded Sol. "Ever hear of *The Invisible Man*?"

"Nope," said Rusty. "Never."

Sol sat down on a chair across the table from Rusty. He took a slow sip from his bottle of Hamm's before saying, "I was an A student in high school. I liked to read a lot. My folks were super proud when I graduated. But I had higher hopes. I wanted to go to college. That didn't work out. But had my senior year, a teacher told me to never stop educating myself regardless of whether I went to college or not. I ended up taking Miss Solem's advice and since leaving high school, I haven't stopped reading. Thus, the books in the bookcase."

Sol got up and took *The Invisible Man* from the bookcase. He sat down again and silently paged through the book.

"I came across Ralph Ellison's *The Invisible Man* a few years ago. It's quite a story."

"What's it about?" asked Rusty.

Sol picked up a pretzel, put it in his mouth, and slowly chewed it. After a sip of Hamm's, he said, "That's not an easy question, Rusty."

"Why's that?" asked Rusty.

"The book's fiction," said Sol, "but it comes off like the main character is a real person describing his life in a memoir. This lead character grew up in the South—I identified with that. He was a really good student—I identified with that too. And he kept getting beaten up by life—that seemed to fit as well. The main character moved away from the South to Harlem. I moved to Detroit—different places—similar situations. The main character continued to find himself in one difficult circumstance after another. However, he never stopped searching for an ally—always tried to find someone who understood him, a person who he could respect. But he ended up getting screwed again and again—sometimes by white folks, other times by Negros. Yet, as he went from one bizarre set of challenges to the next, the main character always kept trying. The book is sort of like an American Negro Odyssey—tells the story of a colored man traveling through the different flavors of American racism. No one seemed to understand the dude—not at all. In the end, the main character decided he was just plain invisible to all of them."

Sol stood up and placed the book back on the shelf. Then he said, "The first time I read *The Invisible Man*, it did sort of seem like my story. The main character was trying so hard to succeed, to do the right things. Yet he was treated poorly—again and again. I was moved by the story. I read it a second time. In fact, I reread it several times, trying to find personal meaning in its symbolism. I finally decided that the stuff that happened to the narrator in Harlem seemed too far out. I mean, it was interesting—but way too extreme. I decided it didn't relate to my life."

Sol took another swig of Hamm's, gazed out his window, and said, "You see, until a couple of months ago, I thought I'd found my place in life here in Motown. But after all that shit went down at the Cadillac plant, the story of *The Invisible Man* came to mind again. I reread the book. It didn't seem far out at all. Like the book's main character, I had tried to do everything right. But my life seemed to be falling apart. I felt isolated—lonely—ignored by all those around me—like it was me who was the invisible man."

Sol said nothing for a minute. Then he continued. "You know, I've made a lot of friends in Detroit. They listened sympathetically when I told them about what went down at Clark. But a few of them gave me the impression that they thought it had been my fault, that I should've handled things differently. Getting fired—that was frightening. I had been sending most of what I earned back to my family. When it began to look like I might end up on the street, I reread Ellison's book. That time, I had no difficulty identifying with the book's narrator."

Sol sighed, then said, "One person I worked with did more than just listen. That was Tex. When he heard what'd happened—and he didn't hear about it from me—he flipped out. I don't know if you've ever seen Tex when he was about to totally lose his cool. You know, he's always so laid back and easygoing. Tex was fighting mad. He told me he wasn't going to stand for it—and he didn't. He raised some kind of hell with our union steward. You know what happened next. Tex got fucked over too. He was thrown out of the Clark Street Assembly Plant with me. It blew me away that a white guy—a Southerner—had turned out to be the one person who would stand up for me. After that, I didn't feel so alone. Tex and I went out for a beer on the day he got his notice. We got stinking drunk. One thing Tex said that evening has been running through my head ever since. *Most people aren't bad. They're just cowards. But there are also evil people out there and you and me—we just ran into a few of them.*"

Sol shook his head as he looked down. "I had been feeling like it's always the Negro that gets the shaft. That's when Tex told me about Ossia—about her life; how she was a victim again and again—how she was treated as if she had no value. Tex told me about you, too; about your life—about your mom's life—and about how you were trying to figure out how to get an education but ended up serving time instead. Tex pays attention to people. He takes their stories personally."

Rusty realized that Sol's insight into Tex was on target.

"A week after we went out for the beers," Sol continued, "I got word from a buddy of mine at the UAW that there were going to be openings at Hamtramck. He told me he would put a word in for me. I told him about Tex, how he'd stood up for me, then gotten thrown out for it. I asked my buddy if he could put in a word for Tex. He told me he would."

Sol picked up another pretzel and took a moment to inspect it before putting it into his mouth and chewing it up.

Then he said, "When I moved into the Green House, I was pretty relieved to have a place I could afford. But nobody here said nothing to me. I'd see people in the halls and we would just walk past one another. I felt pretty invisible. Maybe, that is what it's like for anyone new moving into a place like this. For me, being the only person in this house who's not white, it didn't feel so good. During my first few days here, the only person who spoke to me was Tex."

Sol looked directly at Rusty when he said, "That's why I appreciated you inviting me to go to Tony's along with you. It was the first time anyone visited me here in the room after I moved in. It felt good to be treated like—well—like I belonged here a little bit. And that was the reason I went—

even though I knew I was going to be the only dark-skinned fellow among a slew of honkies at the bar. Your welcoming me made a difference."

Sol paused, then added, "I would appreciate it if you could treat this conversation as sort of private between the two of us."

Rusty responded, "I won't say anything to anyone. But...."

"But what?" Sol asked.

Rusty took a deep breath before saying, "Has Tex said anything about Edith Beaulieu?"

Sol laughed. "Yeah, he did. Seems like some of you people in this place think the house is haunted. Believing in ghosts just ain't my thing."

"Well," said Rusty, "you might have to adjust your beliefs. You're going to learn that there is a ghost—the lady whose husband built this rooming house in the first place back in around 1920. I decided it was a bunch of hooey when I was told about it and ended up having to eat my words. And the thing is, this ghost appears to listen to just about everything that is said in the building. And she sometimes repeats it to others."

Sol laughed again as he said, "I'll believe there's a ghost in this building when she comes up to me and says, *Hi Sol.*"

Sol was standing in between Rusty and the window. He raised his bottle of Hamm's and said, "Still, just to cover all my bases, here's a toast to Ethel, or whatever is the name of this Green House ghost."

Rusty raised his bottle to Sol's toast. After he had put the bottle to his lips, he almost choked on a swig of beer when he saw, standing there in the corner of the room behind Sol, the semi-transparent figure of Edith. Edith Beaulieu was smiling and raised her forefinger to her lips. She was telling Rusty to say nothing. Edith winked at him, then disappeared.

"Yup," Rusty said as he held up his bottle. "To Edith Beaulieu."

Testing

That Tuesday evening, John started the session by saying, "We need to do this right. I've given it a lot of thought and we can't depend on luck. We must be thorough. Using these walkie-talkies, Ossia can sit in the Chevy and warn us if there's a problem. But we need to test them to make sure the walkie-talkie system works. I parked my car a half block from here—about the same distance it will be from the White House. Ossia and I will walk over and I'll leave her in the car and return here. After waiting ten minutes, Ossia will call us on the walkie-talkie and give a practice warning."

John looked at his three housemates and said intently, "Is everyone clear on the plan?"

Tex and Rusty looked at one another, giggled, and shook their heads from side to side.

Ossia, however, said, "Yes," and that was good enough for John.

John and Ossia headed off to his car. As they walked down the hall, Rusty could hear John give directions to Ossia on how to contact them if someone approached the White House while she was on what he referred to as *watch duty*.

"You see, Ossia," said John, "you simply push that button down—no, this button here—not that one—and you talk into the walkie-talkie. You'll be saying something like *Ossia to team; Ossia to Team....*"

After delivering Ossia to his car, John returned to his room and waited along with Tex and Rusty for Ossia's practice call. They sat waiting, but the call didn't come.

After fifteen minutes, John announced, "I am going to go check what's up with Ossia."

John handed his walkie-talkie to Tex and said, "I will test the system in front of Ossia—you know, make sure it's working properly and demonstrate to her how to operate the new communications tool."

John left the room. Several minutes later, John's voice came through on the walkie-talkie accompanied by a lot of static.

"Testing. 1, 2, 3. Testing. This is John. This is John. Can you read me, Tex?"

"Like a book, John. Like a big old fat book."

"Ten-four, Tex. I'm gonna leave Ossia here and return to the room for the actual test."

A few minutes later, John was back in his room with the other men.

"Women," he said. "She hadn't turned the damn thing on. How can she think it's going to work if she doesn't turn it on? I showed her. She's got it now."

A couple of minutes later, The three men heard Ossia's tentative voice accompanied by more static.

"I speak now, John. You hear me? I forget what I supposed say."

"Roger, Ossia. I read you."

"Who Roger, John?" She was quiet for a moment before adding, "What I read?"

Tex took the walkie-talkie from John. He pressed its talk button and said, "You did real good Ossia. We heard you. Now, you can lock the car up and head on back to John's room."

"Lock car? How I lock car?"

John grabbed the walkie-talkie from Tex and said, "Ossia I will come to the car and get you." He paused, then added, "Good job. The test was a huge success."

*****

Once Ossia and John had returned from the car, John informed his housemates that he needed to review the plan for going into the White House. He gave each housemate a copy of a one-page typewritten list. The page was entitled *Plan for White House Caper*. The list included twelve steps.

1. *Go to White House on 12/15. (John drives).*
2. *Ossia remains in car. Men proceed to break into house.*
3. *John rings doorbell.*
4. *If anyone answers door, John explains they are preaching the gospel. He speaks about Jesus for a minute. Then men leave home, return to car; mission is postponed.*
5. *If no one answers the door, proceed with plan.*
6. *Go to north side of house (by the alarm).*
7. *Rusty disables alarm.*
8. *Rusty opens side window.*
9. *Men enter house and go upstairs to back bedroom and up to attic.*
10. *John finds paintings.*
11. *Men leave White House. Exit on northside through same side window (careful to leave everything including doors as they were).*
12. *Go to car and return to Green House.*

After reading the list, Tex, Ossia and Rusty couldn't stop laughing.

"What's so damn funny?" asked John.

Rusty asked, "Do you want me to give a copy of this to the cops, too?"

John gave a befuddled look.

Rusty gathered the four copies of the list. As he tore them up, he said, "John, if we got caught, this magic little list of yours wouldn't have served us too well."

December 15th

When Rusty awoke on the morning of December 15th, he looked out the window and saw an overnight blanket of snow had coated everything.

"Shit," he said aloud. "This is gonna screw up our plan."

Rusty, Tex, Ossia, and John had agreed to meet at the Warren Avenue Diner at nine. By the time Rusty arrived at the diner, the sun was out, the snow had melted and the pavement was almost bare. The others were already sitting in their booth. Rusty greeted them, the waitress came to their table, and the three men each ordered farmer's breakfasts of easy-over eggs, bacon, hash browns, and toast with marmalade and coffee. Ossia requested a bowl of oatmeal with raisins and cream to accompany her tea.

Once the waitress had taken their orders, John cleared his throat, gave an authoritative look to his housemates, and began a briefing. "I got up early this morning," he said. "I wanted to scout out the Silva home,"

He proceeded to open, then slowly read from a little black notebook. "Five AM: Arrived at target house. Home dark except for porchlight and lamp in living room. Seven-thirty: Paper boy delivered paper. Eight-fifteen: Stake-out ending. Lights still on. Newspaper still on porch."

John looked up from his notebook with a self-congratulatory look on his face and said, "There you have it, folks. When we get to Grosse Pointe later, I'll know if anyone's been there based upon whether the newspaper's been taken from the porch or the porchlight and living room lamp have been extinguished. That completes my scouting observations."

Rusty gave an incredulous look at John before saying, "John, you remain an impenetrable idiot. Tear up everything in your fucking little notebook that references this illegal act we are about to commit. Do you realize that if you are arrested, every word you just read to us would be recited out loud to a jury by the prosecutor? I don't give a damn if you end up going to jail. I am concerned, however, for the three of us who are not acting like raving idiots. Tear the pages up, now."

Tex said, "Amen on that on."

Ossia, nodded and added, "John. Not do stupid stuff, today. Please."

John looked at the expression on Tex's face, then on Ossia's and finally on Rusty's. He sighed and said, "OK." Then he proceeded to tear out a handful of pages from his little notebook, rip them into small pieces, and put them into his half-full glass of water.

"There," he said. "Are you happy now?"

Breakfasts were delivered and the housemates focused their attention on their food. After they finished eating, John looked at his watch and said, once again in an authoritative voice, "Time to roll."

The four friends left the diner and walked over to John's Impala Coupe which was parked in front of the diner. They piled in and headed off on their adventure.

****

A half-an-hour later, as they drove past the Silva house, John said, "The newspaper is on the porch. The porchlight and living room lamp are lit. Good signs."

John parked his shiny red Chevy in front of the playground facing south—against any traffic flow—so that, as he explained, "Ossia can easily keep tabs on the house as we men do the deed."

"Let's get it done," John said as he opened the Impala door and stepped onto the pavement. He stood there for a moment holding a walkie-talkie in one hand and Ossia's Kodak Brownie camera in the other before instructing Ossia, "Pretend to read a book while keeping your walkie-talkie turned on and close to your side."

Ossia looked at a thick somewhat tattered copy of *Crime and Punishment* that John had placed next to her and sighed.

"Here," John said handing the Brownie camera to Tex, "I got my hands full with the walkie-talkie. Rusty has to have his hands free so he can do his magic on the alarm and jimmy open the window. You are assigned to carry the camera and you might as well also be the one to take photographs of any weird pieces of art that looks like Edith might have painted them."

Tex took the Brownie camera, chuckled, shook his head, and followed John and Rusty toward the house's front door.

John rang the doorbell. After listening to the chimes and waiting a minute without a response, he headed around to the side of the house. He turned around and indicated with a hand sign that Rusty and Tex should follow him. By the time, Rusty and Tex had gotten to the front corner of the house, John was feeding dog biscuits to Silva's tail-wagging German Shepherd.

Using a screwdriver, jackknife, and needle nose pliers, it took Rusty less than two minutes to disable the house alarm. Six feet away, on the same side of the house, was the double-hung window Rusty had determined could be easily opened. Using his jackknife, he unlatched it and slid open the lower half. Tex gave him a boost and Rusty was inside Silva's elegant study. A moment later, all three men stood in front of a large cherry desk in the room which was lined with floor-to-ceiling bookcases that were crammed with books.

Tex took a photograph of a small painting in the study while Rusty started to open the door to the hall. John signaled Rusty to hold up, whispering to his two housemates, "I want to check out this room."

"What the hell are you thinking?" asked Rusty in an intense, but hushed voice. "Let's get this over with and get out of this place."

"I'm just curious," John responded. "Relax."

John began to examine the documents on top of the desk. Tex, who was standing behind John, looked at the papers over John's shoulder. John opened each desk drawer, one at a time, and quickly perused its contents. He spotted a gold lighter in the top right-side drawer which he placed into his pocket."

"What the hell are you doing?" asked Rusty.

John whispered, "Relax, Rusty. Just Relax."

John opened the file drawer, quickly scanned the folder headings, and pulled out a binder entitled *Confidential Discussions with Bargaining Unit.*

Tex said, "Let me see that," and took the file from John.

Tex spent half a minute glancing through the pages in the file, folded them twice, and put them into his jacket pocket. He handed the empty file folder back to John saying, "Put it back. I am hanging onto the contents. And Rusty's right. We need to get on with this."

John raised his eyebrows before saying, "Okay. Just one more thing."

Then after taking the walkie-talkie from his pants pocket, John pressed its talk button and said, "The team has landed, Ossia. Repeat. The team has landed. Do you read me?"

The static-filled response from Ossia was, "Yes. I hear." She paused and added, "But I not read *Crime and Punishment*, just look at pages."

John responded, "Never mind, Ossia. Just checking to make sure our communications system is working."

John led the other two out of the library. After passing through the kitchen, John got down on all fours and crawled into the dining room. Rusty and Tex followed suit.

They had previously agreed to stay low and move quickly through the dining and living rooms since those rooms' large windows would make them visible to anyone passing the house. However, Tex did stand up to take photographs of each of the dining and living room paintings.

"Pretty damn nice fixings," said Tex. "But Edith's paintings are a little weird. I don't like modern art."

"Let's keep going," said Rusty.

The three men peaked into the sunroom, then returned to the house's entry and tip-toed up the grand staircase, stopping on the landing for a moment to allow Tex to take a photograph of a large oil painting composed primarily of two naked women floating in the sky.

"More of the same," said Tex after snapping the photo. "I just don't understand this stuff. I like traditional paintings a lot—you know, landscapes and portraits. But modern paintings? They just leave me cold."

The three men moved on. At the top of the stairs, John led them into the master bedroom. Its bed was neatly covered with a white, ornately textured bedspread. The bedroom's solid cherry furniture was just as impressive as every other quality piece they had seen throughout the house. A large painting hung over the bed showed a couple making love while seeming to fly through the clouds.

Tex snapped a photo of the painting and said, "Weird."

"Weird?" said John with a big grin on his face. "I would call it Wicked."

Tex rolled his eyes and Rusty whispered, "We need to hustle."

"I gotta take a piss," said John as he went into the master bedroom's pink tile bathroom. His two partners waited. Moments later, Rusty and Tex followed John's example, expelling the results of multiple cups of coffee consumed earlier at the Warren Avenue Diner.

Toilet duties seemingly complete, the three men moved out of the master bedroom to the north side of the second level. They briefly went into the front bedroom. Tex snapped a picture of a colorful silhouette of a woman sitting amongst a backdrop of flowers. Then he photographed the second art piece in that room. It was a framed pen, ink, and charcoal drawing of the Green House.

"Check that one out," Tex said. "I'd love to have that one hanging in my room!"

They moved on, heading past a guest bathroom into the back bedroom. There, Tex photographed a painting of a man and a woman, dressed in white, sitting at a table with a bowl of fruit and a white bird. Meanwhile, Rusty opened the closet door. He was relieved to see, that as Edith had promised, there was a stairway leading to the attic.

It was at that point that John announced, "Sorry guys, I really have to take a crap. I was trying to wait until we got home. But I am in a lot of pain and really have to go."

Without waiting for a response from his stunned partners, John left the back bedroom and headed to the bathroom next door.

Rusty took a flashlight from his jacket pocket and led Tex up the closet stairs into the warm and stuffy attic. He got down on his knees and crawled to the attic's west eve to the spot where Ossia's map indicated they would find the hidden tryptic. It took less than a minute to uncover three two-foot by three-foot wrapped packages. However, Rusty there was also a smaller fourth package wrapped in the same manner as the others.

"I guess we should take this one too," said Rusty to Tex.

The two men moved the four packages to the attic stairway and began to bring them down the attic steps when they heard the toilet flush.

A moment later, an anxious-looking John opened the closet door and whispered to the others, "Heh guys, we gotta be quiet. Ossia just radioed me. A big red car just pulled into the driveway. A man, I'm assuming it's Silva, and a blonde in a fur coat and heels got out of the car. I told Ossia to stay where she was and keep her head down. I hardly had a chance to wipe my ass and flush the toilet before I hurried here to join you. I heard the front door opening as I closed this room's door. I'm hoping they don't go into that bathroom because if they do, they may die from the smell. In any case, we're in deep shit."

Despite their precarious situation, Rusty and Tex couldn't help but start giggling at John's description of the challenge they faced.

"What's so funny, assholes?" whispered John.

Tex, a grin on his face, whispered, "You're the one whose asshole has almost got all of us into *deep shit*. Tell me, John, was taking that crap worth it?"

They heard the front door close and the voices of a man and woman. The three men sat on the attic stairwell steps, straining to hear anything that might forewarn them as to what was going to occur next. They waited, listening closely.

After a short while, they heard a man's voice say, "It was fascinating dining with you at the club today. I enjoyed getting to know you and chatting about art and its importance to humanity. I'm especially pleased you were able to come over and see my art collection. Dan helped me out so much by remaining at the conference in Chicago. The least I could do to pay him back is to show you my art collection."

The woman's voice was slurred. "Dan was absolutely delighted you trusted him to represent the whole Clark Street Assembly Plant at the banquet. When Dan phoned me this morning, he said you asking him to represent the plant this evening at the banquet told him how much confidence you have in him."

It seemed odd to Rusty that they could hear the couple so clearly until he figured out (and shared with Tex and John) that the vent next to where they were sitting on the steps was carrying the voices of the man and woman through the house's heating ducts.

A moment later the woman said, "Gee Mr. Silva, these paintings are so, so, so very imaginative—so colorful. Dan said there wasn't anything special about them. But my gosh, they are simply beautiful."

The man, who they now understood was Silva, said, "CloAnn, please call me Harry. That's what my friends always call me."

"Thank you, Harry," she said, slurring her diction. "I am so impressed with your house so much. And I love your art even more. I am just having a ball—and this bottle of French champagne you just opened—ooh la la! It makes it all even more special."

Silva spoke again. "I have always appreciated the beauty of art, CloAnn—almost as much as I appreciate being around a beautiful woman. Ever since Dan told me about your interest in art, I've wanted to find a time to get you over here."

Their voices were getting louder. Rusty figured they must be coming up the stairway.

Silva said, "That is a really special perfume you're wearing. I have always appreciated the scent of a fine perfume."

CloAnn responded, "It's L'Air du Temps by Nina Ricci."

Then she giggled and said, "Oh, Mr. Silva, you shouldn't be doing that. I am a married woman."

"I'm sorry CloAnn. You are so attractive. It's hard not to pay attention to you."

After a couple of minutes of silence, Silva said, "There is a special painting in the master bedroom. You've got to see it."

"I don't think I should, Harry. I don't think Dan would approve. And I don't want to give you the impression...."

"There was silence for a couple more minutes before CloAnn said, "I really shouldn't have drunk so much at lunch, Harry. But this champagne—oh—it's just really something else."

"You deserve special things, CloAnn. You are a beautiful woman. Here, let me fill your glass."

There was a moment's silence before CloAnn said, "Oh, Mr. Silva. You shouldn't do that. Dan would be furious with both of us."

Silva responded, "Let's keep this as our little secret, CloAnn. Dan will never have to know and I am enjoying being with you so much."

"No, Mr. Silva. This is just not right!"

There was a moment's silence before Silva said, "You are awfully sexy, CloAnn."

"Oh, Mr. Silva. You're such a cad."
*****

Rusty wondered if the couple was in the master bedroom yet. And, if so, would they have shut the bedroom door? Could he and his housemates leave their hiding spot now? Could they sneak out of the house?

All three men jumped when suddenly they heard a woman's voice coming from the top of the attic stairs. The voice had a distinct French accent. It was Edith Beaulieu's ghost.

"Time to go, boys," she said. "They are in the bedroom and the door is closed. It should be safe for you to leave the White House now. But do it quickly and quietly."

The last thing Rusty had expected to encounter in the attic was the ghost of Edith Beaulieu. But after all that had occurred that day, nothing would surprise him. He grabbed one of the three large packages as well as the smaller one and tiptoed down the attic stairway and out of the closet. John and Tex, each carrying one of the packages, followed closely behind him out of the bedroom, through the hall, and down the stairs. When they reached the stairway landing, they heard Silva making a sound that was something between a moan and a howl."

"We need to get the hell out of Dodge," said Rusty.

Tex smiled and whispered, "If you ask me, it's more like we need to get the hell out of Cadillac."

The three men hurried down the rest of the stairs, opened the front door a crack, peeked out to make sure there were no obvious witnesses, and left the home. They walked quickly down the front walk and up the street to John's parked Chevy Impala. Tex and Rusty greeted a much-relieved Ossia while John opened the Chevie's trunk and placed the four packages inside of it. Everyone in the car, John started the Impala's engine and the housemates were on their way back to the Green House.

As John drove his shiny red coupe past the Silva residence, Rusty looked closely at the large home, worrying that at any moment, Silva might come running out of the house screaming at them with a fist raised. But no one came out of the home and the four housemates breathed sighs of relief as John drove them out of sight of the house.

Nothing was said for five minutes.

John broke the silence and caused the others to jump when he almost shouted, "What about the detached alarm? Could that somehow alert Silva to the fact that somebody broke into his house? And the window in the den—did we leave it open?"

Everyone's attention turned to Rusty.

"No problems," said Rusty. "The wire was left dangling inside the box. Someday, when Silva figures out his alarm system isn't working, he'll bring in an electrician who'll figure that whoever attached the wire last hadn't tightened the screw sufficiently. And the window—I closed it and latched it after we got into the study."

John gave a sigh of relief and said, "I suppose someone could just break into that house, now—I mean the way we did—and there'd be nothing to holding him back. Am I right?"

"Yeah, I guess he could," Tex replied. "But that guy would have to be a total idiot—who was willing to give up all his friends forever. Don't get any fancy ideas, John. If Edith hadn't suddenly appeared, we'd probably still be up there sitting on the attic steps, sweating it out."

Twenty minutes later, John parked his shiny red Impala a half-block from the Green House and the housemates removed the four wrapped packages from his trunk. As they carried their found treasures back to the Green House, Tex asked, "Now, what are we going to do with these paintings?"

The three men turned to Ossia. She shrugged her shoulders and said, "Edith meet with us tomorrow evening. You come my room at seven. I serve tea. She tell you then."

An Interesting Debrief

Rusty arrived at Ossia's room ten minutes before the agreed-upon time for the housemate debrief with Edith. For once, he would not be the last one to arrive. However, when Ossia opened the door, John and Tex were already sitting on the settee, drinking tea and chatting. Being the last to arrive, Rust was again relegated to a stool.

The three colorful unframed canvases that had been retrieved the previous day were leaning against Ossia's window. The compositions seemed to be as Edith had described them. While the housemates waited for Edith, they studied the tryptic and sipped oolong tea.

Precisely at seven, Edith's soft voice addressed the group. "*Bon soir, mes amis.* Thank you for all you did for me yesterday. After Ossia returned to the Green House, I asked her to open my lovely hidden packages. Upon seeing them, I was overwhelmed with a joyous flood of wonderful memories from my youth."

Edith became visible. She was standing in front of, and looking at, the storied canvases. She turned to the four housemates with a look of joy on her face and said, "Yesterday, I was thrilled to discover that whatever makes this world spin, once again, transported me to my beautiful Chateau Blanc. Before warning you to leave, I toured my cherished home and refreshed many happy memories. And, like you, I was shocked by the callous behavior of the home's current owner. He is indeed a crude and selfish *cochon.*"

Edith Beaulieu stopped speaking, turned to the tryptic, and studied the three paintings.

Then she turned to the housemates and said, "Ossia told me you are interested in knowing where I wish to display the tryptic. I have given this a great deal of thought. The Detroit Institute of Art owns several of my canvases that they display with their Twentieth-Century American Art

Collection. I will ask my beneficiary, Jeannine to approach the museum. If they are interested, she will contribute the tryptic to their collection. No one will question whether Jeannine had possession of them since my passing I believe the museum will be pleased to accept and display them."

Edith looked back to the four housemates and asked, "Does that work for you?"

They nodded their assent.

At that point, John asked, "What was in the fourth package, Edith? Where is it now?"

Edith gave a soft laugh before replying. "I asked, Ossia to open that package as well. So many years ago, I hid an envelope with a Ford Motor Company stock certificate next to the tryptic. The stock shares it represented were given to me by my husband shortly after we married. He laughed when he handed me the gift saying it was a dowry in reverse. Edwin told me the certificate was quite valuable and that I should put it away for a rainy day. I kept it below my nighties in the bottom drawer of my dresser. When I decided to hide the tryptic, it seemed like a good idea to keep the Ford certificate in the same place. Over the years, I forgot about the stock. But sadly, the certificate is now only a worthless piece of paper—an interesting souvenir from another time. I am certain it has no value. Unfortunately, everything my husband owned became worthless when the stock market crashed."

"Could I see the certificate, Edith?" asked John.

"Yes, of course," was the ghost's quick reply. "Ossia— please collect the envelope for John."

Ossia walked to her dresser and returned a moment later with an aged envelope which she handed to John. He opened the envelope and carefully removed a yellowed certificate with an ornate border. The top half of the certificate featured an engraved eagle with *Ford Motor Company* printed above it in large bold type. The lower half of the certificate was an engraved form upon which names, dates, number of shares, and dollar amounts had been handwritten in ink.

John read the certificate aloud. *"This certifies that Edwin Byerly is the owner of twenty-five shares of the capital stock of Ford Motor Company transferrable only on the books of the Corporation by the holder hereof in person or by attorney upon surrender of this certificate properly endorsed."*

John studied the certificate for a couple of minutes, then continued to describe it. "At the top of the certificate, it says *Capital - $2,500*. At the bottom, it says *25 Shares*. The certificate has Ford Motor Company's corporate seal and is hand-dated June 26, 1903. It is hand signed by James Couzens, Ford's secretary, and Ford's president John Gray."

There was silence in the room before Edith said, "As I said, this piece of paper has no value, John. Edwin lost everything he owned on Black Tuesday—the day he...," She sucked in her breath, then blew it out, saying, "the day he died."

John kept studying the document. Then he turned to the ghost of Edith Beaulieu Byerly and said, "Don't be so certain, Edith, that the certificate is without value. Maybe, you're right; but maybe not. My dad was an investor during the crash. I remember him telling me he bought some corporate stock at a huge discount in 1930 or '31. I think it was Proctor and Gamble's common shares. His colleagues told him the stock was worthless. But the shares did eventually regain their face value. I need to do some checking on your certificate. Can I hold onto it for a few days? I'll touch base with an attorney I trust who used to work for my family. He'll be able to tell us if the stock has any value."

Edith's ghost responded, "Of course. But don't hold your breath waiting for it to have value."

"Thank you," said John. "I won't hold my breath. But I am hoping the certificate does have value. I will let you all know as soon as I learn anything."

Rusty interjected, "Speaking of things lifted from the house, John, what's the story with your appropriating that gold lighter out of the desk? If any of us are ever arrested, that lighter would become some pretty compelling evidence of theft."

John's face turned red as he mumbled. "I didn't think anyone noticed."

"Here," John said. He pulled the lighter out of his pants pocket and held it out for the others to see. "This whole escapade seemed like one of the coolest things I'd ever been involved in. I thought the lighter would be a cool trinket to keep—you know, sort of like a personal souvenir. Maybe someday in the future, I could pull it out and tell somebody—maybe it would be my grandchild or maybe my girlfriend. I'd tell them how I'd ripped the lighter off during this elaborate home robbery—and they—whoever I was showing it to—they would be impressed. Taking it—like everything else that happened during the visit to the White House—now seems like it was a whole lot more complicated than I appreciated at the time."

John placed the gold lighter on the table. Ossia turned the lighter on its side. The others leaned forward to see it, then sat back in awe. Engraved in rolling script on the side of the gold lighter was, *To Edwin with love, from your ever-loving Edith.*

Ossia whispered, "Edith, you need look, see."

Edith's ghost glided over to the table and looked at the golden object. The others watched the ghost as silent tears rolled down her cheeks.

"It was our tenth anniversary," she said. "Things were good then. Edwin took me to New York City to catch George Gershwin's "Lady Be Good." Afterward, we went out to Keen's Steak House for dinner. Edwin had a juicy New

York cut. I had a tender filet. We drank an expensive Bordeaux and got pretty tipsy. Edwin surprised me at the end of the meal by giving me a beautiful pearl hairpin from Tiffany's. Then, I surprised him with this gift of a gold lighter, also from Tiffany's."

Rusty asked, "What do you want us to do with it, Edith? I don't think any of us should keep it."

Edith was silent.

Ossia said, "Let Edith consider. I hold now."

John picked up the lighter and meekly handed it to Ossia. She put it in the pocket of her housecoat.
*****

Rusty, Ossia, John and Edith looked at Tex.

Tex looked at his housemates and quietly said, "Yup. I read your look and I guess it's my turn. When I saw that file folder named *Confidential Discussions with Bargain Unit Rep,* I was suspicious. After opening the folder and seeing my name along with Solomon's in the document's first paragraph, I knew I wasn't leaving it there. Once we were back in my room, I read it over—several times."

"And?" said John.

Tex shot a contemptuous look at John before continuing. "*And,* John, the words I read gave me confirmation that my local's bargaining unit officers are two-faced, lying, sons-of-bitches. They agreed to a bullshit deal with management that stated Sol and I had and, wait, I got the exact wording here."

Tex took a folded piece of notebook paper out of his shirt pocket. He unfolded it and read from pencil-written notes. "*These workers aggressively and continually worked to increase racial tensions in the facility by falsely accusing co-workers and supervisors of racist behavior with the intent of creating conflict between white employees and colored assembly line workers.*"

Rusty had never seen Tex so angry.

Tex continued, "And get this. The goddamned agreement says *These employees were warned more than once to discontinue this behavior. They ignored directives to stop inciting racial conflict between and among their co-workers.*"

Tex took a deep breath, then slowly let it out before saying, "In exchange for accepting that pack of lies, our local president got a couple of his buddies rehired—good old boys who'd been fired in October for submitting false timecards. Everyone at the plant knew that neither Sol nor I had done anything wrong. But we got sold out in exchange for bringing back a couple of maggots who deserved to be fired in the first place."

Tex stood up and walked to the window, looking out into the cold, windy night.

A moment later, he turned back to Rusty, John, and Ossia and said, "My local shop president is as racist as Silva. Both of them would probably be happy if they could get rid of every colored worker in the place. If any union leader outside of the local president found out about this, they would be just as angry as I am right now."

"Is there anything you can do about it?" said Rusty.

Tex looked out the window for a moment. "That's what I've been noodling, Rusty, ever since I saw the agreement. I should be able to do something with it. But I gotta figure out what can be done and how. I want to be careful not to get us into trouble for stealing the document from Silva's place."

Tex stopped talking and began to chuckle.

"What's so funny?" asked John.

"What's so funny? The document said that Dan Norton, Clark's personnel manager, was the manager who the document says warned Sol and me not to cause trouble. He even signed as a witness on the damned agreement. Dan Norton is probably the husband of CloAnn—the woman

Silva was fucking when we were in the house. It seems like Silva was screwing everyone—one way or another!"

John laughed and said, "You just can't make this stuff up."

Tex gave a thoughtful look before saying, "Until I figure out how to deal with this, I'm not gonna say anything about it to Sol. Depending on if and how we use the agreement, I want to make sure he can't be accused of being a part of its theft."

Unexpected Visitors

Monday afternoon, as Rusty walked home from Grace Hospital, he thought about the bizarre series of events that had unfolded during the weekend. Jeannine's door opened as he entered the Green House. She had a serious look on her face.

"Rusty. We need to talk."

"Sure, Jeannine," he responded and followed her into her small apartment. He worried that this was it—he was finally going to get kicked out of the Green House.

However, when he entered Jeannine's apartment, Rusty saw Ossia was sitting on Jeannine's couch. Behind her stood the semi-transparent figure of Edith Beaulieu.

After Rusty sat down on the couch next to Ossia, he asked, "Has something happened?"

Jeannine sat down on a chair next to the couch and said, "I often gaze out my front window when I sit here drinking tea. At about ten this morning, a big black Chrysler pulled up in front of the Green House. It had *Detroit Police* printed on its front door in large yellow letters. A uniformed policeman and another man wearing a dark suit got out of the car. They came up to our front door and knocked. I went to the door and asked them how I could help. The man in the suit showed me a badge and introduced himself as Detective Chet Whitley with the Detroit Police Department. He asked if John Nygren lived here. I told them, *Yes, he does.* The detective said that they wanted to speak with John. Was he home?"

Rusty looked at Ossia. Based on how red her eyes were, he knew she had been crying. And behind her, the ghost of Edith wore a look of concern.

Jeannine resumed speaking. "I told the police detective that I did not know if John was home, but that I would take them to his room—which I did. After John answered my knock on his door, the detective introduced himself and told John he wanted to ask him a few questions. Then he turned to me and said I could leave. The detective and the police officer followed John into his room and the door closed. I returned to my apartment—quite worried. Half an hour later, Detective Whitley and the officer came downstairs with John. John's hands were secured behind his back with metal bracelets. The police led him out of the building, seating him in the back seat of their black police car."

Ossia took over describing of the day. "Then Jeannine come my room; tell me police take John. I tell her everything—Edith want paintings—about Saturday—Tex and John break in White House—man and woman come—take packages and leave."

Ossia bit her lip and looked down at the floor before saying, "I afraid. Give Jeannine gold lighter."

After Ossia had said this, she, Jeannine, and Edith gave a pleading look at Rusty. But Rusty just sat with a stoic look on his face. Flashing through his mind were visions of returning to the state prison. All Rusty could say was, "Shit."

The three people and the ghost waited in Jeannine's apartment. A fidgety hour later, the front Green House door opened. Tex and Solomon Smith had returned from their day's work at the Hamtramck Assembly Plant. As they entered the Green House, Jeannine opened her door and asked Tex to come into her apartment. Solomon continued up to his room.

Once Tex was in Jeannine's apartment, Jeannine and Ossia repeated their description of the morning's events.

Tex responded identically to Rusty. "Shit," was his only comment.

The two women, two men, and the ghost waited in the apartment for something to happen. Around 5:30, Jeannine served ginger tea and butter cookies. As the group munched on cookies and drank tea, each person wore a grim expression. Even Edith paced back and forth, saying nothing and occasionally looking out Jeannine's window as if expecting John to suddenly appear.

Ossia put her anxious feelings into words. "You think police come—arrest us—take us away? I worry so much for this. What if they take citizenship from me—send me back Poland? I live so many years—a prisoner. This must not happen, not now—not again—never, ever—must not happen."

Tex tried to soothe her fears. "Ossia, they can't take away your citizenship. And we didn't do anything so bad. And you, Ossia, you didn't break in. You just sat in the car."

However, the look on Tex's face betrayed his own fears. He took a deep breath and glanced at Rusty as if hoping for some confirmation of his statement.

Rusty just looked down at the floor. He didn't want to put words to the fear that was running through his body. He didn't want to return to prison. Rusty figured the others would get off with probation. But Rusty, an ex-convict—he was the one who had disarmed the alarm system, the one who had broken into multiple homes in the past. Rusty would be the two-time offender. He would be the one to pay the price.

After an hour of silence, Ossia said, "Never have trouble America police. Think maybe call lawyer?"

Rusty looked up and said, "We need to be patient, Ossia. We have to remain cool. John may be a jerk, But he's an awfully smart jerk. I don't think he will screw this up."

He paused, then added, "Maybe I need to be more honest and use the words *hope and pray he won't screw it up.*"

Another mostly silent hour passed. Jeannine told the others she would fix a snack. Minutes later, she carried a small tea tray to the coffee table. On it were four wine glasses, an open bottle of Bordeaux, a plate of crackers, and a dish that held several wedges of cheese.

Jeannine poured red wine into each wineglass. Rusty noted that this was the first time he had seen Ossia consume an alcoholic drink.

After taking a small sip of wine and making a face that communicated how much she disliked the wine, Ossia said quietly, "Not like wine taste. But today, I need."

Rusty raised his glass and said, "To John staying cool."

His housemates raised their glasses and repeated, "To John staying cool."

Tex took a bite of a cracker which he had generously loaded with blue cheese. "Stinky cheese!" he said. "I hate stinky cheese!"

He paused; took another bite; then added, "Today this stinky cheese doesn't taste so bad. Thank you, Jeannine. Thank you for the wine and the food. I was hungry enough to eat a bear—so the blue cheese was OK. Anyhow, it tasted a whole lot better than raw bear."

The housemates began to watch the pendulum on Jeannine's wall clock swing back and forth as the clock's minute hands slowly crept forward. The chimes that signaled the quarter hour seemed to cry out, "John isn't home. It's getting late."

At 9:30, Rusty had had it. "I gotta go up and turn in," he said. "I have to be at work early tomorrow morning and need some shut-eye."

Tex said, "Likewise," and stood up.

The two men were moving toward Jeannine's door when Ossia pointed out the window. Headlights swept by and a black Plymouth pulled in front of the Green House. The car had *Detroit Police* printed on its front door. The tension in the room jumped when a uniformed Detroit police officer emerged from the squad car and walked around the car, toward the house.

But the officer continued to walk around the patrol car until he reached its back door which he opened. A moment later, John stepped out. John and the officer spoke for a minute, shook hands and the officer returned to his vehicle. John watched as the black squad car drove off.

A moment later, John entered the Green House and after Jeannine summoned him, he sauntered into the apartment.

Tex, Rusty, Ossia, and Jeannine looked worried. Even Edith seemed tense. John, on the other hand, looked totally at ease. He chuckled when he saw the group waiting for him. Jeannine brought a chair over from her small dining set and asked John to take a seat.

John, a twinkle in his eye, said, "Don't I get a glass of that wine too?"

Jeannine went to her small kitchen counter, opened another bottle of Bordeaux and brought it and an empty wine glass to the coffee table. A moment later, John's glass was full and the other four glasses had been topped off.

"Thank you," said John before tasting the wine.

After making a show of swishing the wine around in his mouth, then swallowing it, John gave a nod of approval to Jeannine and said, "Good stuff, Jeannine. I should visit you more often."

John sliced off a thick piece of Brie cheese and placed it upon a cracker. As the others watched, John took a big bite, chewed it slowly, rolled his eyes, and gave a big smile.

Ossia anxiously asked, "What happen John? Where you go? We in trouble? Maybe arrested—deported?"

"I'll answer those and other questions," John responded in a patronizing manner. "But I want to do this in my own way. I will write about this huge adventure someday. But today, I can't—for obvious reasons. So let me enjoy this."

*****

Then John began to narrate his tale.

"I was innocently reading *Crime and Punishment* this morning when there was a knock on the door. If you've never read Dostoevsky, let me share with you that his stories are always intense. But in *Crime and Punishment,* Dostoevsky makes the reader feel like they committed the murder."

At this point, Tex interrupted John. "I don't give a damn about your review of some Russian murder mystery, John. Get to the point. What happened?"

John looked at the ceiling, gave an exaggerated sigh, then continued. "I opened my door and there was Jeannine, standing next to a cop and another guy in a suit. I admit I was worried. I wasn't ready for any kind of punishment—crime or not. After Jeannine was asked to leave, the two men came into my room. The suit told me he wanted to ask a few questions. I think my response was, *Shoot—But please don't use your guns.* I chuckled. Neither the suit nor the cop even cracked a smile."

None of the housemates gave a positive response to John's cute attempt at humor.

Rusty said, "I agree with Tex, John. Cut out the bullshit."

John continued in the same Dashiell Hammett *whodunnit* tone. "The suit did all the talking. He flipped a badge at me and introduced himself as Detective Whitley. Whitley told me the Grosse Pointe police had received a complaint from a homeowner. They, in turn, called the

Detroit cops asking for assistance with an investigation related to the homeowner's complaint."

John sipped his wine, sighed, and continued. "Whitley asked me about my whereabouts over the last few days. When he said *the last few days* rather than specifically *Saturday,* I guessed he probably knew I had been at Silva's house but didn't know when. If that was the case, I deduced that he probably didn't know if I had been there with anyone else. I decided that since he hadn't told me anything, why should I tell him anything? I replied *I spend most of my time in my room writing, detective. But I do go out occasionally. When are you asking me if I was out of my room?"*

John took a large bite of his cracker and cheese. He chewed it thoroughly before getting back to his story.

"Whitley wasn't giving up," John said a moment later. "He got more specific and asked if I'd been to Grosse Point in the last few days. I asked him why he was asking."

John took a sip of wine and said, "This wine really is outstanding, Jeannine."

Jeannine impatiently said, "Keep talking John. If you don't get to the point quickly, I will take that glass of wine in your hand and toss it into the sink."

"OK," he said. "Whitley didn't like me—I figured that much out. He said *I'm asking if you've been to Grosse Pointe.* I responded; *I'm asking why you're asking.* Then the detective got a little ahead of himself and told me a Grosse Pointe homeowner had found my wallet in his guest bathroom. When I heard this, my thought was, *Shit, I've screwed this all up.* Whitley continued, *We want to know how that wallet got there, Nygren. Since we are not getting anything done here, I am going to have to take you to the station and ask you my questions there. Maybe a less comfortable environment might loosen your tongue a little."*

John took a deep breath, let it out slowly, and said, "Next, he read me my Miranda rights. Now, I've watched

Peter Gunn and *Dragnet* often enough to know that that's not a good sign. After reading me my rights, he turned to the uniformed officer and said, *Sergeant—cuff the jerk.* If Whitley's goal had been to make me uptight, he had succeeded. On the other hand, I wasn't going to let him know that. But what could I do? Jump out my window? Anyway, the cop went ahead and put the handcuffs on me and marched me down to the squad car."

John stood up. He started walking around the room, carrying his glass of wine and occasionally taking a sip while continuing to tell his story. "It took about half an hour to drive to the precinct station. When we arrived at the station, they took me into a little room. The sergeant left and Whitley asked if I wanted a cup of coffee or a cigarette. I told him, *Yes on the coffee; no on the cigarette.* He left the room and returned with two cups of horrible reheated coffee. He started to take out a Camel cigarette. I asked him if he could refrain from smoking because I had had asthma as a kid. Now I admit, I made that asthma thing up then and there. But unless he had my medical history, he didn't know that. After I said that, Whitley rolled his eyes and put the unlit cigarette back into the pack of Camels. Then Detective Whitley asked me if I was ready to make a statement."

At this point, John chuckled before saying, "By now I was fully prepared. I'd used the half-an-hour ride to the station to think the whole thing through. During that time, I remembered something my Uncle Harold once told me. Harold said there are three elements to the truth. First, there's the truth. Second, there's the whole truth. And third, there's nothing but the truth. My Uncle Harold tied the three together for me by saying, *In a pinch, you should always tell the truth. But,* Harold added, *you might not want to tell the whole truth.* And then Uncle Harold concluded with the magic elixir, *In a tough circumstance, do not limit yourself to saying nothing but the truth.*"

John took another sip of wine and chuckled. "So, I told Detective Whitley, *I actually was in that home across from the lake. It was on Saturday. I know I shouldn't have been there, Detective. But I left my wallet. The guy found it. And now I have to admit to you, yes, I was there.*"

At this point, Ossia started to cry. Jeannine gave her a Kleenex.

John continued, "*The reason I was in that bathroom,*" I told Whitley, *was because I needed to take a crap.* Please notice that up to this point, I had been following the first element of Harold's advice. I was telling the truth. At that point, I moved on to part two of Harold's advice. I refrained from telling him the whole truth."

John looked at Ossia as he said, "Ossia, I didn't mention that I was there with anyone else or tell him why I was there. Instead, I moved right into the third element of Harold's advice. I began to tell Detective Whitley things that weren't entirely true. But I sprinkled my lies with fragments of truth. *I'm a writer,* I told Whitley. *I'm about to write a book about Edith Beaulieu, an immigrant from France who became an outstanding painter in the Detroit area and died about a decade ago. Edith lived with her husband Edwin in that Grosse Point house into which I walked. I, on the other hand, live in a rooming house that Edith and her husband built, a building in which Edith lived for the last two decades of her life. Edith Beaulieu was a marvelous painter. I wanted to see her home. My plan had been,* I told him, *to knock on the door and ask whoever lived there if I could look at some of Edith's paintings which I understood were still in the house.*"

Edith's ghost expressed her appreciation of John's statement. She smiled and said, "If you want to write that book someday, John, I would be delighted to assist you with the details. You might want to tell a little bit about my parents. My father helped me develop the philosophy that guided my painting and my mother taught me about color."

John smiled, thanked her, and replied that he would most definitely ask for her assistance. Then he went back to narrating his story. "I continued to elaborate on the truth. I told Whitley *When I arrived at the house, a Cadillac was sitting in the driveway. I guessed someone was home. I walked up to the front door and could see from the inscription on the door that the homeowner's name was Silva. That was when I saw that the front door was partway open. While I didn't see anyone, I could hear a conversation quite clearly. It was between the guy—I learned it was Silva—and a woman whose name I figured out was CloAnn Norton. It seems CloAnn is married to a guy named Dan Norton—an employee of Sylva's. Dan had been sent off by Silva to some conference in Chicago and CloAnn was drunk. She talked about how she had been drinking champagne at lunch with Silva before arriving at the house and she thanked Silva for opening another bottle of champagne after they got to the house. I have to tell you,* I told Whitley, *that this woman was quite drunk and Silva was working hard to get her into his bedroom. Apparently, CloAnn liked art and Silva kept telling her he wanted to show her the painting above his bed. I can only imagine why that painting was such a big attraction.*"

As Rusty listened, he began to realize that John had done a brilliant job of embellishing the truth without changing it—too much. Rusty began to relax, took a sip of wine, and decided to enjoy John's elaborate patter.

"By now," John went on, "Detective Whitley was into my story. So much so, he forgot to interrupt me with questions. *Up to this point,* I told him, *I had done nothing wrong. I had listened to a conversation between a couple of people who were about to have sex. But I was still outside the door which they had left open. I hadn't even touched the door knob. I told Whitley, I did something thing you probably will think is a problem.*"

John stopped speaking and poured himself some more wine. Jeannine watched him pour it and the irritation on her face was unmistakable. After filling his glass, John took a sip, closed his eyes, and savored the taste.

Then John set the wineglass down and said to what was now his audience, "So I told the detective, *Based upon what I'd heard, I figured that Silva and CloAnn must have gone upstairs. So, as long as I was there, I decided I should just take a quick look at Edith Beaulieu's paintings on the first floor. Yes, Detective, I went into the house. I moved pretty quickly because I didn't know how long it was going to take before Silva finished seducing CloAnn. And Beaulieu's paintings were simply amazing, Detective, absolutely captivating. I sincerely regretted I hadn't brought my camera. I was on my way out of the house when I looked up the stairway and there, hung on the landing, was a wonderful oil painting. I walked up to it and gave it a quick look over. But when I looked up at the second floor, I realized there were more paintings upstairs. I could hear Silva still working on CloAnn and figured I had at least a couple more minutes. So, I hustled up the stairway and quickly looked at the paintings in the rooms on the side of the House opposite where Silva was working on CloAnn. Then something bad happened."*

John shook his head and said to his housemates, "I should have been a con man. Whitley was eating it all up and furiously writing down everything I said. I told him, *What happened was I had to take a crap. I know, Detective, that that was a horrible time to have to have a bowel movement. But it happened and I was standing in front of a bathroom and I was certain I would be able to take care of my business really quickly."*

By now, Tex and Rusty were laughing.

John continued to revel in his oral fiction. "I told Detective Whitley, *I took that crap so fast, Detective. Then I got the hell out of there. As I left the house, I heard a man's screaming moan. I don't think Silva was angry. I think he was just giving sound to some animal emotion he had while screwing Mrs. Norton. Anyway, I had no idea that my wallet had popped out while I sat on the toilet. And the truth is, Mr. Detective, I know I shouldn't have gone in there. I understand that that is probably against the law. And it was definitely a dumb move to have gone to take a crap there. But I really had to go—awfully badly. Anyway, I hurried out of the house after that and I'd done no harm. I took nothing and my intent was not bad in any way."*

John had a grin on his face as he said, "Anyway, when I finished my story, Detective Whitley gave me a long look and said, '*Young man, you have broken the law. Going into a home without the owner's permission is a serious misdemeanor. I need to check with Mr. Silva before charging you with a crime. Doing that will require him to press charges.*'"

John had his housemates, building manager, and the Green Houses' resident ghost leaning forward, waiting to hear what happened next. John stopped speaking, allowing the suspense to build.

Finally, Tex said, "And...."

"*And*, my friend," said John with a sinister smile, "*And* I ended up laying there on a jail cot, resting in the police jail cell for a few hours. I was sharing the cell with a couple of gentlemen. One of them was in there for lewd conduct; the other for shoplifting. When I became hungry, I politely asked the guard for something to eat. Half an hour later, he brought me a tray with a pretty good turkey and lettuce on rye. I've had better—but not in jail. The vanilla pudding—it was quite good. The apple juice was ok. The coffee? I already told you about it. It was awful."

It was obvious John was enjoying being the center of attention and, given the fact that it didn't seem like anyone else was going to be arrested, the others allowed him to drag out his moment in the spotlight.

"So finally," John said, "finally, Detective Whitley returns and says to me, *Well, Mr. Nygren, you're one lucky fellow. Mr. Silva must be a very nice guy because he has decided he's not going to press charges.* The detective was smirking. I think he understood what Silva's issues were. Then he added, *I can tell you for certain we've got all of this documented and you had better watch your step in the future because next time, you might not be so lucky.*"

John finished up with a flourish. "I wasn't surprised about the outcome. I had given my story a lot of thought while they drove me to the station—and I do think I am an awfully good storyteller. I was confident Silva wouldn't press charges because it would turn the whole thing into a public record establishing the fact that he'd seduced his employee's wife. And even though I don't have that gold cigarette lighter to show in the future when I tell somebody about what a cool thing I'd done, today's interrogation just made my story that much richer. Maybe I'll write a book about this whole set of events—someday—maybe—in fifty years."

After John finished, Jeannine went back to her dresser, opened a drawer, and returned.

"Here," she said, "you are a great storyteller. You've earned this."

Jeannine handed John the gold lighter he had stolen from Silva's desk a couple of days before. Then Jeannine, the ghost of Edith Beaulieu, and John's three housemates stood up and gave John Nygren a standing ovation.

The Stock Certificate

A couple of weeks later, John asked Rusty, Ossia and Tex to meet him for a Saturday breakfast at the Warren Avenue Diner. He wanted to update them on his research into the Ford Motor Company bond certificate.

That Saturday, sitting in their familiar booth at the diner, the men ordered farmer breakfasts with coffee and Ossia ordered a bowl of hot oatmeal and a cup of herbal tea.

After the waitress had taken their orders and returned to the kitchen, John said, "After Edith gave me the go-ahead, I checked in with the attorney. I asked him about the value of the Ford Motor Company stock certificate. He told me he needed to do some research and would get back to me. He contacted me this week and explained his delay by saying that the issue had turned out to be more complex than he'd anticipated."

"And?" said Tex in a sarcastic manner mimicking John's previous snotty comment.

"*And,*" continued John, "here is what I learned. When Henry Ford started Ford Motor Company in 1903, he needed capital to get the company rolling. To get that funding, he sold stock to some local investors. Byerly bought twenty-five shares at $100 per share. In 1919, Henry Ford decided to keep the highly successful automobile company private. He initiated a buyback of the stock issued in 1903. Each share that had been purchased for $100 per share in 1903 would be bought back by Ford in 1919 for $12,500 per share—125 times its original price! Edwin Byerly's twenty-five shares had gone up in value from $2,500 in 1903 to $312,500 in 1919."

"That's a shitload of profit. Did Byerly sell the stock or did he miss out?" asked Rusty.

"Hold on to your horses," said John. "In 1919, all investors were given the option of taking a cash payment from Ford. For Edwin and Edith Byerly that amount would have been $312,500. However, certificate holders were given a second option—taking an equivalent value of General Electric stock. Investors were notified that any investor who did not respond to Ford's offer to purchase the stock would have their Ford shares automatically converted into GE common stock. What took the attorney so long was to figure out if Byerly had gotten a cash payment from Ford in 1919."

Tex laughed, "We're talking serious history now. You're searching to find a check that would have been written before the roaring twenties!"

"You're right, Tex. That's why the attorney had to go to General Electric and that is why the GE folks had to do a bunch of their own research. GE finally did get back to the lawyer this week. Apparently, Byerly never responded to the 1919 notification. We don't know why. Bottom line, Edwin's shares of Ford stock were converted into General Electric stock."

"Certificate still have value?" asked Ossia.

"It does," responded John. "That's what's so damn amazing. Each share of GE common stock had a value of a little over a hundred dollars in 1919. Its value went up during the 1920s, then it crashed in 1929. But the company survived the Depression and the value of its shares has since increased."

"What are they worth now?" asked Rusty.

"At this point," replied John, "the GE shares awarded to Byerly are worth more than six times what they were worth in 1919. Those shares that Edwin gave to Edith, that she tucked into that envelope and hid in the attic—they're worth almost two million dollars!"

There was a deafening silence at the table. A couple of minutes later when the waitress brought the housemates their breakfasts, they had still not spoken a word. The four housemates ate their breakfasts in stunned silence. Nothing was said until after the waitress had cleared the last cup, plate, and spoon from the table.

Ossia asked, "Edith and Edwin dead. Who get money?"

"The attorney said a court would have to decide," said John. "He guessed, however, that the money would go to Jeannine. She was Ossia's only heir. I asked him if there was any chance that the two million bucks could be treated as sort of a finder-keepers' reward. He said he doubted it."

"I speak with Edith," said Ossia quietly. "She dead, true. But she, well, she...."

Ossia was silent for a moment before saying, "I speak with Edith."

Legal Strategies

A couple of weeks later, Tex told John, Rusty, and Ossia that he had invited Sol to join them for their next breakfast at the Warren Avenue Diner.

That Saturday, the housemates sat at a table instead of their regular booth. After pleasantries and breakfasts had been ordered, Tex began the update. "In our first conversation about the labor-management agreement, I said we shouldn't speak with others about my taking the document from Silva's desk. Since then, I wasn't able to figure out how to use the document in a way that accomplished anything. So, earlier this week, I broke down and told Solomon about the break-in into Silva's house."

He stopped speaking when the waitress came to the table and refilled their coffee cups and Ossia's tea cozy.

Once the waitress left, Tex continued. "I told Sol how we came across the labor agreement but explained I couldn't figure out how we could use it. Sol listened and then made some suggestions. I figured they made sense. I asked him to have breakfast with us today to share his ideas with you. Sol, can you take it from there?"

Sol took a deep breath, slowly blew it out, and began to speak. "Tex came down to my room the other evening and filled me in on your—what should I call it—your adventure. My first reaction was to wonder what the hell you'd been smoking. After I read the agreement, my focus changed. I'd known that our local president and Silva were both racist. But I was surprised they were dumb enough to document it. And, I gotta admit, I was blown away when Tex told me that Silva had nailed the wife of his personnel manager after I saw that the guy had lied in the document on Silva's behalf.

That was another proof to me that loyalty at Clark only runs one way."

Sol gave an embarrassed look at Ossia and said, *Sorry for the vulgarities, mam.*

Ossia laughed and said, "But it accurate, Solomon."

"Anyway," Sol went on, "when Tex asked how I thought he should approach this whole thing, I had a good idea of what to suggest. You see, I probably have a few contacts you folks don't."

Solomon Smith stopped speaking as the waitress set down farmer's breakfasts in front of the men and a bowl of oatmeal in front of Ossia.

After the waitress had refilled their coffee cups and Ossia's tea cozy, Sol continued. "I know an attorney, Marcella Brown, who volunteers with the NAACP. She's trustworthy and pretty smart. She might have a suggestion or two on how to deal with this whole thing. If you guys want me to get in touch with her, I'll do it."

Tex added, "If Sol and I don't capitalize on this agreement, we've let the bastards off the hook. On the other hand, if it got out that we busted into Silva's house, you guys would be in just as much trouble as me. So, It's gotta be a group decision. What do you think? Do we want Sol to contact this lawyer?"

Rusty, John, and Ossia looked at one another for a moment.

John spoke first. "Sounds like a good plan. I just want to make sure that nobody learns how we got a copy of the agreement. The cops already know I was in the house."

Rusty nodded. "I'm on board, too. And, John is right. Maybe you could show her a Xerox of the agreement instead of the actual document?"

Ossia added, "Yes."

Tex said, "OK, Sol. Go ahead. Set up a meeting for me and you with this attorney."

"I'll get ahold of her as soon as I can," replied Sol.

With that, the housemates dug into their breakfasts.
*****

Tex touched bases with Rusty a few days later. "Sol contacted the attorney. She's gonna meet Sol and me at her office on Saturday morning. I'll bring a Xerox of the agreement. I've already told John and Ossia."

"Good luck." Rusty replied, "Keep us informed—and out of jail."
*****

Saturday evening, the five housemates walked together to Tony's Bar. While they walked, Sol provided an update on the meeting with Marcella Brown.

"Tex started it out by telling Marcella how each of us got fired. Then he handed her a Xerox of the agreement. Brown read it and reread it. Then she asked us how we got ahold of it. I told her we couldn't share who gave us our copy of the document. She didn't question that."

John asked, "Is that all?"

"Relax John," said Tex. "We'll get there."

Sol continued. "Marcella said it was unusual to have a UAW local agree to anything like that. UAW leadership has been pretty progressive on racial issues. We told her about Silva and the racist crap he's pulled off again and again. Brown said she actually remembered hearing stuff about Silva in the past. Apparently, he's played fast and loose with a lot of people."

Tex laughed and added, "Then she added that Silva's been on thin ice with the auto workers for years and this time, he just might end up going through the ice into the lake."

"Toward the end of the meeting," Sol said, "Marcella told us that if we authorized her, she would call someone she knew with the United Auto Workers' Civil Rights Action Committee. If the UAW got on board, she might be able to set up a meeting with General Motors. Marcella thinks we should try to settle this without going to court. She thought the UAW and GM would prefer to get it resolved without publicity."

Tex took over. "Then Marcella asked us what sort of resolution we wanted. Sol and I had never talked about what sort of fix we wanted other than getting back at the assholes who screwed us. Sol told her getting fired had cost him the financial benefits of seniority and that all of the folks he used to work with had been told he was a troublemaker—that bothered him a lot. I agreed with Sol that those were the things we wanted fixed. Marcella asked us if we wanted to go back to work at Clark Street. I told her I guessed so. But I was concerned that Silva would find a way to get back at us."

Sol concluded the update. "Marcella told us not to worry about Silva. She figured he would end up getting what he deserved. She told us she'll get back to us in the next week or two."

Follow-up

It was early February. The five housemates hadn't had any new updates on the Clark Street labor agreement in over a month.

Rusty ran into Tex in the Green House hallway as Tex was returning from work.

"Marcella Brown sent Sol a note asking him to call her," said Tex. "Sol returned the call during lunch break today. She updated him on everything that has happened with the UAW and GM. Sol and I want to fill you, John, and Ossia in on everything this evening. We're going to meet at Ossia's room at seven."

*****

When Rusty arrived at Ossia's room, John, Sol, and Tex were already there. John had brought a six-pack of Budweiser and handed a bottle of Bud to Rusty.

Ossia said, "Sol and Tex. We all here now. What you learn?"

"OK," said Tex. "After we gave Marcella the go-ahead at the end of December, she contacted an NAACP lawyer and went over everything with him. He agreed they should go to the auto workers' union. At that meeting, the UAW attorney told them he had to speak with the Clark Street local's leadership council. He needed to get their side of the story. It took several weeks before the UAW got back to the NAACP and Marcella."

"This is where it all got interesting," said Sol holding back a smile. "The old local president hadn't shared the labor-management agreement that got us fired with anyone in the bargaining unit. The UAW attorney told Marcella that after the local membership found out about what had gone down, new officers were put in place at the local. Then the UAW attorney called someone at General Motors to discuss the situation."

John's comment was "Wow."

Sol continued, "General Motors got back to the UAW and the NAACP this week. Marcella said GM didn't give a whole lot of detail about how it happened, but Silva had been fired and General Motors has agreed that Tex and I shouldn't have been fired. They're offering us full back-pay for November, December, January, and February and giving us the month of March as paid vacation."

"Double wow," said John. Then he paused and added, "Are you going to accept? You know, you could go after more."

Tex responded. "Are you kidding, John? Sol and I each thought we were going to end up broke and on the street. Now, with what we earned at Hamtramck and the retro check, both of us are financially ahead! And the vacation? That means I get a whole month with my family. Do you realize how long it's been since I have spent a month with Ginger? How could I turn that down?"

Sol added, "I wouldn't think about turning it down either. That'll be the biggest check I've ever seen. And having Silva and that son-of-a-bitch former union president pay for their behavior—oh, that's so damn sweet. Marcella came through for us."

Tex lifted his still, half-full bottle of Budweiser into the air and said, "Here's to Marcella."

Rusty added, "And here is to happy endings."

Another Get-Together

Jeannine invited Sol, Tex, John, Ossia, and Rusty to her apartment for wine, cheese and crackers on Sunday, February 21st. That was a week before Tex and Sol planned on leaving on their Greyhound trips home to visit their families during the month of March.

When Rusty arrived at Jeannine's apartment, Tex, John, Sol, and Ossia were already seated with full glasses of wine. Jeannine's coffee table was loaded with crackers and Cheddar, Swiss, and Brie cheeses. As Rusty sat on a dining room chair next to the couch, Jeannine handed him a glass of red wine.

John said to Jeannine, "This is an exceptional wine. To what do we owe the pleasure of such a feast?"

"I imagine all of you have been wondering that," said Jeannine. "The truth is, this soiree wasn't my idea. Edith asked for us to get together."

At that point, Edith Beaulieu's semi-transparent apparition slowly appeared and appeared to sit on the third dining chair.

Edith said, "Hi Sol. Others have told you about me and I know you doubted my existence. Now you know they were telling you the truth.

Sol had a look of total shock on his face.

Ossia, Tex, John, Jeannine, and Tex smiled. Those smiles turned into a chorus of tension-relieving laughter in which Sol was a solid participant.

"Over the past few weeks," said Edith, "Jeannine and I have spoken a great deal about the proceeds from the investment certificate my husband Edwin generously gave to me over a half-century ago."

There was silence in the room.

Edith looked at the housemates' glasses and said, "Jeannine, our guests' wine glasses are empty. Could you please bring over a second bottle of that Chateau Lafitte Rothschild and fill their glasses? I think they'll need it."

After the wine was poured and tasted, the group's attention returned to Edith.

"Sol," Edith said, "I know your housemates shared with you that they retrieved a Ford Motor Company stock certificate that has turned out to be quite valuable. What Jeannine and I are about to do is to explain how the proceeds will be used."

Afterward, Sol laughed as he told Rusty he was in shock at having a ghost speak to him. At that point in the evening, all he was able to get out was a weak, "Uh huh. Yes, mam."

"John," Edith said, "Thank you for having the Ford stock certificate researched and for giving your attorney's contact information to Jeannine. Jeannine reached out to him and the attorney confirmed that Jeannine is the beneficiary and that the value of the investment certificate is over two million dollars. Jeannine asked him if he would work as her attorney to help address several issues related to that certificate. He agreed to do this."

"He's an excellent attorney," said John.

Edith continued. "Jeannine and I feel that some compensation is due to each of you for breaking into the White House on my behalf. She has asked the attorney to draw up paperwork that shares the proceeds."

It was like the air was sucked out of the room.

Edith's voice was quiet and measured as she said, "Jeannine will, of course, be the major beneficiary. She will receive half of the proceeds after taxes and legal expenses. The remaining amount—except for fifty thousand dollars will be divided evenly between Ossia, Tex, Rusty, and John. Thus, each of the four of you will receive over two hundred thousand dollars. I have no doubt you will find good uses for those funds."

The look on the faces of Ossia, Tex, Rusty, and John was sheer amazement.

"Jeannine has chosen to not remain here at the Green House," Edith continued. "Our attorney has purchased—on Jeannine's behalf—a large white brick Georgian-style home in Grosse Point. It is a lovely home with a grand view of Lake St. Clair. The home—and all of its contents was recently put up for sale after the automobile executive who had lived in it was discharged by his employer. This man has since moved from the area."

Edith turned to Ossia saying, "Jeannine told me she did not want to live in that large home by herself. Ossia, Jeannine would like you to share the home with her."

Ossia's jaw dropped. Then she covered her face with her hands and wept.

"As for me, said Edith, "I cannot stay in the Green House without my dear niece or my lovely Ossia. I am hopeful my spirit will be transported to the White House as well."

And Jeannine began to silently cry.

"Sol," Edith continued in a quiet, business-like manner. "When Henry Ford started his company, he depended upon people from the deep South to come to Detroit and build cars for his company. I have always been aware of how people of color were treated as second-class citizens. I was guilty of that myself. I lived in this building for many years and while I was aware of the unfair treatment toward people whose skin was dark, I surrounded myself with people whose skin color was closer to my own. Jeannine continued the practice I initiated of renting rooms only to people whose skin tone was light. When you told Rusty about some of the disgraceful behavior you endured in Detroit—at work and away from work—I listened and was ashamed—totally ashamed."

Sol's face displayed a look of bewilderment as Edith continued. "Sol—I was wrong and Jeannine was wrong." She paused, then said, "The Green House has been good to me."

Jeannine added, "And it has been good to me as well."

Edith looked directly at Sol as she said, "Since Jeannine and I will be moving to that beautiful White House along the shores of Lake St. Clair, someone needs to own and manage this wonderful boarding house into the future. If you are willing, Sol, Jeannine will direct our attorney to transfer the title of the Green House to you. Of course, there will be maintenance issues that come up. The fifty thousand dollars I mentioned earlier will be placed into your checking account to make sure you have the required resources to deal with those challenges—and of course, to assist you in providing support to your family down South."

Edith's ghost appeared to take a deep breath. "So, if this works for all of you," she said as she looked briefly at each of the faces in front of her, "if everyone accepts my plan, then Jeannine will direct our attorney—thank you again, John, for recommending him—to initiate the actions I have described."

There was a befuddled silence in the room. Tears continued to roll down Ossia's cheeks. Jeannine gave her a handkerchief. A moment later, Jeannine needed a handkerchief herself and soon after that, it was obvious that Tex had a similar need. Jeannine crossed the room and returned with a box of Kleenexes from her kitchenette.

To no one's surprise, John was not at a loss for words. "Edith. You are amazing. We are grateful for your generosity, humbled by your approach, and exuberant for one-another. I am sure I speak for every one of us when I say thank you."

"Thank you, John," said Edith. "That is our plan. Jeannine—would you please bring out that third bottle of Chateau Lafitte? I think our guests are thirsty."

Happy Endings

A couple of months after the Green House residents' sale of just over two million dollars of General Electric stock was complete, Rusty resigned from Grace Hospital. He enrolled as a full-time student at nearby Wayne State University and continued to live in the Green House until he received his bachelor's degree in the spring of 1967. At that point, having been accepted into a Master of Social Work program at the University of Michigan he moved to Ann Arbor, and out of the Green House. Once Rusty had received his master's degree, he secured a position as a counselor at Innovation Central High School in Grand Rapids, Michigan. There, Rusty, his wife (whom he had met while studying at Wayne State) and their children lived happily ever after.

Tex took his planned vacation home to the panhandle of rural Texas. When he returned to Detroit at the end of March, he resigned from the Clark Street Assembly Plant and returned to Texas. Using his share of proceeds from the sale of the GE stock, Tex was able to pay off the mortgage on his home and land and purchase a small tavern in the nearby town of Hutchinson, Texas. Tex was his tavern's primary barkeeper. However, every Friday and Saturday evening, Tex performed two sets of country and western music for his bar's patrons. Tex's wife attended every one of those performances.

At the end of April, Ossia moved with Jeannine (and Edith) into the Grosse Point White House. The home's sunroom became her artist's studio. Over the next few years, Ossia's colorful and mysterious paintings developed quite a following in the Grosse Point area. The Detroit Institute of Art ended up purchasing several of her works.

Tex gave Jeannine a toy poodle whom she named Odilon. Together, she and Odilon went for many joyous walks along the waterfront of Lake St. Clair. Jeannine also spent many hours sitting with Edith in the living room admiring Edith's paintings and sharing happy memories of their youths growing up in the City of Light.

John approached Jeannine shortly after the General Electric stock sale was finalized. He told her he intended to continue writing and asked if he could rent the back bedroom in the White House. Of course, she gladly agreed. During the next few years, John spent most of his time in the White House study where he wrote five mystery novels about the paranormal. All five were successfully published.

Solomon Smith stayed on at the Clark Street Assembly Plant. He married a co-worker he had met during his stint at Dodge Hamtramck. Sol's wife quit work just before their first child was born in 1963. Later that year, Solomon converted two rooms on the first floor of the Green House into an expanded living space for his family. The remaining first-floor room was used by Solomon's mother after she came to live with her son's family a year later.

Solomon continued to rent rooms to tenants on the second and third floors of the Green House. Workers of diverse colors who didn't happen to have family in the Detroit area found a sense of belonging within that three-story boarding house.

Sol and Rusty became close friends. Sol liked Rusty's plan to pursue a college degree so much that he decided to enroll in an occasional class at Wayne State University. In the fall of 1964, Sol left the Clark Street Assembly Plant and took on a full courseload at Wayne State with an emphasis on history and education. After receiving his bachelor's degree in 1968, he began a career as a history teacher at Detroit's Frederick Douglas Academy High School. Sol taught there, inspiring young folks, until his retirement.

The bonds that began at the Green House remained an important touchstone in the lives of Rusty, Sol, John, Tex, Ossia, Jeannine, and yes, even Edith Beaulieu. Each Thanksgiving, this group of friends along with their families gathered at Jeannine's Grosse Point White House to celebrate their wonderful friendship.